A PROPOSAL
FROM THE
CROWN PRINCE

A PROPOSAL
FROM THE
CROWN PRINCE

BY

JESSICA GILMORE

First published in Great Britain 2017
By Mills & Boon, an imprint of HarperCollins*Publishers*
1 London Bridge Street, London, SE1 9GF

Large Print edition 2018

© 2017 Jessica Gilmore

ISBN: 978-0-263-07327-0

MIX
Paper from
responsible sources
FSC   FSC™ C007454
www.fsc.org

This book is produced from independently certified FSC™ paper to ensure responsible forest management. For more information visit www.harpercollins.co.uk/green.

Printed and bound in Great Britain
by CPI Group (UK) Ltd, Croydon, CR0 4YY

To my very own hardworking ballerina.

I hope one day you really will be
a tree in Covent Garden. xxx

CHAPTER ONE

POSY'S CHEEKS ACHED but her smile didn't waver, nor did she flinch as a bead of sweat rolled down her forehead, another trickling slowly down her back. Her muscles screamed for release but she kept perfectly still, one leg bent, an arm outstretched, head high, eyes fixed on the cheering crowd. They were on their feet, shouts of 'bravo!' reverberating around the auditorium as bouquet after ravishing bouquet were carried onto the stage to be laid reverentially at her fellow dancer's feet.

What must it feel like to be Daria, Posy wondered as Daria kissed her hand to the ecstatic audience, to know that all this rapture was for you? How did it feel to star in a brand-new ballet, choreographed just for you, and to have London at your feet? She and Daria had started ballet school together years before, had once stood side by side, the only two girls from their year to make it into the Company—but now Daria shone right in centre stage while Posy remained firmly in the heart of the Corps de Ballet.

But there was still hope, the promotions were yet to be announced. Maybe this year she would finally make Artist and be given some of the smaller featured roles—and then First Artist to Soloist and on and on until she reached the exalted rank of Principal. Maybe...

But at twenty-four, five years after she'd graduated into the Company, it was getting harder and harder to keep hoping. Of course, she reminded herself as another bead of sweat trickled down her cheek, thousands of people would kill for the opportunity to be doing exactly what she was doing, would consider being able to dance in nearly every production of the most prestigious ballet company in the world enough in itself. But it wasn't enough; she wanted more.

Posy stayed backstage longer than usual after the curtain finally fell, standing quietly to one side of the cavernous room as the rest of the dancers exited chattering excitedly and the stagehands began to move the scenery back into its designated space. There was always an extra buzz after a Saturday night's performance, adrenaline mixing with the sweet knowledge there was no class on a Sunday so the dancers could flock to their favourite Covent Garden haunts, filling the tables vacated by the tourists as night drew in. But Posy couldn't shake her flatness and so she waited until the backstage area had cleared before making her way out. When she finally reached the dressing room she shared with several other girls it was empty apart from the usual bottles of make-up and brushes scattered on the dressing tables, discarded tights and pointe shoes piled in the corner and costumes hanging on rails, waiting for the costume department to collect, clean and mend them before the next performance.

Posy sank into her chair with a sigh, avoiding her own gaze in the brightly lit mirror. She didn't want to see the sweat-streaked stage make-up accenting her eyes, cheekbones and lips, the dark hair twisted into the bun she had worn every day for years, slim but muscled shoulders and arms, the clavicles at her neck clearly visible. Her make-up itched, felt too heavy, claggy on her skin, her shoulders ached and her ankles twinged. As for her feet, well, she knew all too well that it was her job to smile and look effortless while *en pointe*, that it took as much practice to smile through the pain as it did to perfect a pirouette, but tonight her shoes pinched more than usual, the ribbons too tight around her ankles. It took a few moments to undo the knots and slip them off, pulling off her toepads to reveal the bruised and blistered feet of a professional ballet dancer. She winced as she flexed her feet. Every twinge was worth it. Usually…

'You look *triste, chérie.*'

Posy jumped as a voice floated over from the door; she'd assumed all her friends had left. She forced a smile and turned to greet her fellow Corps ballerina. 'Hi, Elise. No, I'm fine. Just end-of-season blues, the usual.' The principals and soloists were heading out on an Australian tour before stepping into a series of lucrative guest artist appearances but the summer always seemed longer and emptier for those without international reputations. She usually filled her break with stints teaching at summer schools, extra classes and courses and trying to find opportunities to perform wherever she could. She knew she was luckier than many ballet dancers—at least she was paid over the summer months—but she still felt lost at the thought of weeks without her usual routine of classes, rehearsals and performances.

The diminutive French girl sauntered into the room and dropped gracefully into the chair next to Posy's. 'Me, I'm looking forward to the break,' she said. 'I thought you were too. Don't you have a holiday home to visit?'

Posy shrugged. She knew she should be more excited about the house her godmother had left her but her recent visit to the rambling pink villa on L'Isola dei Fiori for her sister Miranda's rather sudden wedding had left her filled less with the thrill of home ownership than with panic. The villa was huge and had obviously once been beautiful but now it was dilapidated, the garden still overgrown despite her sister Immi's best efforts, with walls literally crumbling down. It was going to cost a fortune to put right—and a fortune was something she most definitely didn't have.

'I am planning to go there at some point over the summer, but my sister's there at the moment and I'm not sure how long she's planning on staying.' The villa did have an immediate use—it had been a bolt-hole for all three of her sisters; first Miranda, then Portia and now Imogen had all fled there to try and regroup in a year that seemed full of upheaval. Posy knew she was being silly, there was no reason she couldn't stay there at the same time as her sister, but years away at ballet school had left her feeling very much the outsider in her own family. It didn't help that the sisters nearest in age were twins, neither of whom had wanted to spend much time with the baby of the family when they were growing up.

'If I had a villa on the beach I would be heading straight there and possibly never coming back.'

Elise eyed Posy keenly. 'Unless there's another reason you're staying around.'

Posy shifted in her seat, unpinning her hair so she didn't have to meet Elise's gaze. 'I don't want to be too far away. People are ill on tour, they need emergency understudies; I'd hate to miss out because I'm not here.' She just needed the opportunity to stand out. If they would just give her a solo, one small role, then they would see what she could do.

Elise didn't answer for a long moment; instead she swept the discarded hairpins up from Posy's dressing table and began to bend them back into shape. 'Posy, you and I have danced together for how long now? Three years?'

Posy nodded, her chest tightening at Elise's unusually serious tone.

'In that time neither of us have been asked to do anything extra, to be featured in any way while girls who joined this season, last season, have been getting duets, solos, character parts.'

Posy closed her eyes. It was all too true. 'It doesn't mean we won't get there...'

'*Non,*' Elise contradicted her. 'It does. And I for one did not become a dancer to spend my life being nothing but beautiful scenery.'

'What do you mean?'

'I'm leaving. I'm joining a tour company.'

Posy spun round and stared at her friend in disbelief. 'You're what? Cramped dressing rooms, digs, a different small town every day, no paid holiday? Instead of here, instead of all this history, the reputation? Why?'

'To dance,' Elise said simply. 'I will go in as First Soloist, if I do well then I could be Principal by this time next year. I have been promised a chance to dance Clara and Aurora this autumn. There's even a chance of Odette/Odile if I work hard. I deserve this. I've paid my dues here, Posy. As have you. Why don't you come with me? I know they would jump at the opportunity to have someone with your training.'

But Posy was already shaking her head. Here was where she was meant to be. This was the stage she wanted to conquer—not a different stage every night. 'I can't. But I wish you all the luck in the world if this is what you really want.'

'What I want is a handsome prince to whisk me away from all of this, but if it won't happen in real life at least I'll get to dance it. Posy, there's a whole world outside. Remember that, you have choices…but come, it's Saturday night and we are free for such a short while. Do you want me to wait for you? There's a table at Luigi's with our name at it.'

'You go ahead. I'm still not changed and I left my jacket in the studio. I'll see you there, okay?'

'Okay. Don't be too long. It's not good to be alone when your thoughts are sad.'

There's a whole world outside. Elise's words echoed through Posy's head as she headed away from the dressing room and up the staircase that led to the rehearsal studios and break rooms where she spent much of her day. There *was* a world outside but this was all she had ever wanted from the moment she first put a ballet shoe on. She had sacrificed friends, romance, higher education, even her family to be able to walk along these corridors, rehearse in these studios. To step out onto that stage. How could she give up on her dream when it was still attainable? Impossible.

She'd expected the dancers' area to be dark and shut up but to her surprise the lights were on in the wide corridors. She stopped to look at the familiar space, at the sofas lined up along the wall facing the huge windows with their views across Covent Garden and the wider city skyline, encouraging the dancers to sit and rest between their gruelling routine of class and rehearsal. Windows above the sofas looked into the large studios, each wall covered with mirrors and barres, capable of holding forty or so dancers. She spent nine hours a day, six days a week in these corridors and studios; they were more home than the narrow bedroom she rented just a few streets away.

She'd left her jacket slung on one of the sofas and she picked it up, suddenly impatient to be out of the building and away from her worries. Elise was right, maybe being alone when she was sad was a mistake. She'd be better off at Luigi's with

a glass of wine and a plate of pasta, her usual
Saturday night treat. As she turned she caught
sight of two people in the studio and froze when
she recognised the ballet master, Bruno, and the
formidable company director, Dame Marietta
Kirotsova, deep in conversation.

Her heartbeat speeded up. Here was her chance,
handed to her on a plate. She could go in there
and ask them just what she had to do, what she
had to work on, how she could distinguish herself enough to finally take her rightful place as a
featured artist. She inhaled, apprehension creep-
ing through her. She was used to criticism, to re-
jection; she had to be. But this time it mattered
more than it ever had.

'Just move, Posy,' she admonished herself, but
for the first time in her life her feet wouldn't
obey. Maybe she was a coward after all, maybe
it was better to hope than to know that there *was*
no hope.

And then all thoughts fled as she heard her
name, loud and clear through the partly opened
door. She tried to speak up, to let them know she

was there, but her voice had dried up, her limbs incapable of movement.

'Rosalind Marlowe? Oh, you mean Posy?' Bruno's voice, still heavily Italian even after several decades in London, carried easily through the still air. Posy swallowed, wishing she were anywhere else.

'She's danced with us for five seasons. Do you think she's ready for a featured part?'

Posy squeezed her eyes shut, wishing with all the fervour of a small child for the right answer, that her worries would all be over soon.

'No.'

And just like that her world ended.

'She's an excellent technical dancer, maybe the best we have. I can see her as *coryphée* one day—and she would be a wonderful teacher. But she doesn't have the fire, the passion to step outside the corps. I never look at her in character and believe this is a woman who has loved, who has lived. It's a pity but as I say she is almost unsurpassed technically and a great asset to the company...'

Posy didn't wait to hear more. Somehow she regained control of her legs and began to back quietly away. She had her answer. She would never be a soloist, never stand in the spotlight, never see the crowds jumping to their feet for her. Worse, she would never dance the steps she knew and loved so well. Would never be Juliet or Giselle. She was fated to watch other girls live out the tragedies. She had failed.

CHAPTER TWO

NICO MIGHT—AND DID—tell himself that he would rather be anywhere in the world than stuck here on L'Isola dei Fiori but even he had to admit that right now he was as contented as an imprisoned man could be. Maybe it was the soft summer evening light, the way the brilliance of the sun had dimmed to a glowing warmth, the sea breeze a cool accent to the heat. Maybe it was the scent of night-blooming jasmine mingling with the salty tang of the sea or maybe it was the way the green cliff tops rolled across the horizon dipping suddenly into the azure blue of the sea punctuated only by the curving perfection of fine white sand.

So, maybe L'Isola dei Fiori felt like a prison but at least it was a beautiful one and as he strolled along the cliff path towards the Villa Rosa it was easy to forget all the reasons he didn't want to be here—and all the reasons why he was tethered to his island home.

Although the nearest beach was technically open to anyone, like all the beaches on the island it was Crown property; the only known path to it led from the fading pink villa, majestically poised on the very edge of the cliffs looking out over the sea. The only known path to those who didn't know every inch of the island by heart, that was. And Nico did. Whether he liked it or not every path, every bend, every slope, every blade of grass and grain of sand was emblazoned on his heart, in their own way as binding as his obligations.

The way was hidden by two boulders, seemingly impenetrable unless you knew the exact turn—a smart right, almost turning back on yourself, a squeeze and then the path lay before you—more of a goat trail than a formal path, a steep, twisting scramble down to the beach. Nico stared down at the overgrowth covering much of the rocky path. How many times had he raced Alessandro down here, half running, half slithering onto the beach below, only to return bruised, scraped and exhilarated from another forbidden adventure?

His eyes burned. No, he wouldn't think of Alessandro. But it was hard not to when every corner held a twist of nostalgia, a memory to cut deep. Two years on and time had healed nothing. Grimly he increased his speed, the adrenaline of the fast clamber down chasing away his grief in a way no other attempt at solace had until he finally half leapt, half fell down the last vertical slick of rock onto the sand below. Nico kicked off his shoes, the soft sand beneath his toes anchoring him firmly back in the here and now.

It had been over a decade since he'd last visited this particular cove and nothing seemed to have changed. Nico had travelled to more than his fair share of stunning places but on an evening like this the secret cove was hard to beat: small but perfectly formed, the sand curving in a deep horseshoe partitioned by a graceful arch of craggy rock. The waves lapped gently on the shore and Nico knew from experience that the currents were kind, the water deepening gently, several long strides before a bather found himself thigh deep.

The summer breeze was lessened down here, the steep cliffs providing a natural shelter, and Nico realised how warm he was, his T-shirt sticking to his torso. He eyed the sea, already feeling the coolness of the water against his heated skin. It wasn't that late and the fierceness of the day's sun would ensure the water was a pleasurable temperature—not that he and Alessandro had ever cared about the time of year or day, as happy to night swim in winter as they were in summer, the sea their eternal playground, until Alessandro had grown up, grown into his responsibilities and put their boyhood adventures firmly behind him. For all the good it had done him...

And now it was Nico's turn to shoulder the burden, to take his responsibilities so seriously he would no longer be able to sneak away for an evening swim. Really he shouldn't now; the sensible thing would be to turn around and go home. He clenched his fists. *No*, he had a lifetime of making sensible decisions ahead of him, a lifetime of duty first, self last. Tonight belonged to him. To the memory of two young boys sneaking away from tradition and responsibility to bathe by the light of the moon.

His body decided before his mind was fully made up, shucking off his damp T-shirt and stepping out of his shorts and boxers, leaving them in a crumpled pile on the sand as he walked naked towards the welcoming sea. It was only as his toe touched the refreshing water that he remembered the main reason why this was a bad idea. Nico paused briefly then shrugged the thought off. If a paparazzi was so enterprising as to follow him here then he or she would get the shot of a lifetime. His mouth curved as he pictured his uncle's reaction. It would almost be worth it…

The water was every bit as revitalising as he had hoped, the waves not too strong, the temperature warm at first, turning more bracing as he headed out into the deeper waters. He struck out with strong, sure strokes, out, out and further out until, when he turned to float lazily on his back, the beach was just a smudge of yellow. He stayed there for some time, happy to just scull gently in the water as the waves broke over him, rocking him from side to side, the late, sinking sun still warm on his salt wet face. It was hard to imagine ever being this free again when tomorrow he would formally take up his duties, his future one of ceremonies and meetings, a hidebound, indoor, rigid existence.

And, sooner rather than later, a wife. A family. A suitable consort chosen for him.

At the thought his buoyant mood sank quicker than a pebble thrown into the water and he was back on his front and striking back to shore, not with the bold freedom of his earlier strokes but with a precise, weary determination, fighting his own instinct to flee as much as the outgoing tide.

He was closing in on the beach, his pile of clothes coming into focus, when he saw her. Nico stilled, swearing under his breath as he slowed to tread water.

She was on the other side of the arch that bisected the beach into two, standing near the narrow jetty and the natural thermal pool that made the beach so famous. He couldn't see her boat but, seeing as she had just stepped off the jetty, he was betting she had moored on the other side. If he was careful then Nico might be able to make his way to shore and grab his clothes and be out of there before she noticed him. Or he could stay here, bobbing up and down like a seal and wait for her to leave. Neither option appealed but action would always win out over inaction. So stealthy approach it was.

His mind made up, Nico looked over at the girl again. She was too far away for him to make out her features. All he could see was a petite, very slim frame topped with a mass of long dark hair. She kicked along the beach, hands in pockets, staring down at the ground. Everything about her suggested despair and Nico felt a pull of kinsmanship. He was about to move off when she stopped, straightened and flung back her hair, curving one elegant arm above her head and executing what seemed to him to be a perfect pirouette on the beach. She paused and then spun round again and then again, hair flowing, like some beach naiad performing her evening rites.

Nico sensed that he was intruding on something intensely personal yet he couldn't look away, transfixed by the grace and agility so unselfconsciously displayed, and by the time she drew her white dress over her head in one fluid movement and dropped it on the beach it was too late to turn away, to swim away. She wasn't wearing a bra and it took less than two seconds for her to step out of her knickers and walk into the sea with the same grace she had displayed as she had danced.

She must be a naiad or a siren and he, like Odysseus, was caught, too mesmerised to retreat. All he could do was wait and hope that she wouldn't see him. A futile hope—Nico knew the moment she spotted him because she stopped dead in the water, spluttering as a wave caught her unawares. It was his cue and he swam a little nearer, not too close, not enough to alarm her any more than he already had. 'Nice evening for it.'

If looks could kill he would be shark meat,

his dead body right now slipping underneath the waves. 'I thought this was private property.'

His mouth curved appreciably. Her head was held high as she trod water, her dark eyes fierce. 'The sea? Are you Poseidon's princess to claim ownership over the waves?'

She swallowed, visibly fighting for control. 'The beach. The beach is private property.'

'It's not, you know,' he said conversationally. 'It's property of the Crown, open to all, and even if it wasn't you, mysterious naiad, aren't a Del Castro.' That he was confident of; he knew every member of the most distant branches of the royal family tree.

'But there's only one way down and that *is* private property.' She tossed her head as she spoke, triumph in her voice. 'And I know you didn't come by boat.'

'There's always another way, if you know where to look.'

'Were you watching me? Just then?'

'Not on purpose,' Nico admitted. 'The beach was empty when I got here so, really, I should be the offended one. You intruded on my privacy, not the other way round.'

She didn't answer his teasing smile. Instead her brows shot up in rejecting disdain. 'A gentleman would have drawn attention to his presence.' She managed to convey affronted dignity despite the hair floating around her pale, naked shoulders, the drops shimmering on her eyelashes.

'Ah. But I'm no gentleman. Ask my uncle. Besides, I didn't want to draw attention to my presence. I am also…erm…in a similar state of undress.' His smile widened as her cheeks flushed.

'I think you should leave immediately.'

'But I don't trust you not to peek.'

She glared at him. 'Believe me, I've seen it all before.'

'This is a predicament.' Nico moved closer. He was enjoying himself more than he had believed possible. If she'd shown any real signs of anger or fear he would have swum out of there with an apology but, for all her outraged words, there was a spark in her eyes that told him she was enjoying the verbal sparring as much as he was. That maybe she too relished the opportunity to forget her worries, to feel alive. She was younger than he had first thought, early to mid-twenties, her creamy skin a contrast to her large dark eyes and almost-black hair. She wasn't exactly beautiful but there was something arresting about her features, a striking dignity that made him want to look twice and then again. 'You and I here, our clothes there. I'm really not sure what our next move should be.'

That wasn't entirely true. He *was* sure what he wanted to do—but not if he should. He wanted to swim closer, next to her. He wanted to see if those eyes darkened even more with desire, wanted to taste that plump bottom lip. He wanted to forget that tomorrow he would be presented with a list of suitable wives and expected to pick one with as much thought as he gave buying a new phone. He wanted to lose himself in another human being of his own choosing while he still could. He wanted to live on his last night of freedom.

* * *

She should be outraged. Possibly scared. Definitely wary. This man had plainly been watching her—watched her dance, watched her strip, watched her wade naked—*naked*—into the water. He'd lounged here insolently invading her privacy. And now, instead of apologising and leaving her to her evening swim, he was looking at her as if…well, as if he wanted to eat her.

She *should* be outraged but the clench deep down wasn't fear; nor was the tingling in her arms and breasts. Posy took a deep breath, her legs suddenly weak, treading water as she fought to hold onto her composure. 'Our next move?' she managed to say, keeping her voice level. 'There's no "our". You are going to swim back to your clothes, I will swim back to mine and neither of us will turn around or acknowledge each other in any way. Understand?'

His smile didn't waver, a confident, amused grin, which infuriated her almost as much as her body's traitorous reaction to the play of muscles across his shoulders and to the heat in his navy-blue eyes. 'If you insist, naiad.'

'Don't call me that.'

'But what else should I call a fair maiden dancing on the shore before slipping into the waves? A mermaid? A siren—or are you a selkie? Waiting for me to leave before slipping into your seal skin?'

'Don't be so silly and you don't need to call me anything…' She paused, embarrassed that she was reacting so strongly to his teasing, her innate good manners forcing her to add, 'But if you did need to, then my name is Posy.'

'Nice to meet you, Posy. I'm Nico.'

'I wish I could say the same but I didn't actually want to meet anyone tonight.'

'Me neither,' he admitted and, startled, she looked directly at him, her prickles soothed by the lurking smile in his eyes. 'This is a place one comes to for solitude, isn't it? I didn't think anyone would be here. If I had I would have packed some trunks.'

'Yes.' She wasn't sure what she was agreeing

with—the joint need for space and to be alone or that swimwear was a good idea. 'Okay then. Now we've been introduced let's call an end to this impromptu meeting. I propose that you go that way, I go this.'

'Deal. I hope you find it, whatever you came out looking for tonight.' He paused, his eyes intent on hers for one long moment, before turning and with a graceful dive, which gave Posy a glimpse of a tanned, lean torso and a decent pair of legs, he powered off towards the opposite side of the beach. She lingered, watching his strong body cut through the waves for one guilty second before turning and kicking off in a more sedate breaststroke back to the beach, glad of the cool water on her overheated flesh.

Posy was no stranger to gorgeous male bodies—she spent most of her time with physically perfect specimens clad in Lycra and tights, every single muscle perfectly defined. She was used to being lifted and held, spun and moved, her partner's hands moving with sure possession over her body. That was why when she dated, she dated within the company. Men from outside could never understand that when her partner's hand clasped her inner thigh the last thing either of them was thinking about was sex. A dancer's body was public property; there was no room for coyness. She was used to nudity, to being nude—or as good as. To react so strongly to the knowledge of another person's nakedness was foreign to her. She hadn't been able to see much. They'd both been cloaked by the evening sea. But she'd known, she'd reacted—and that discombobulated her.

Also, she was a fool. She should have swum away the second she noticed him. She was lucky he wasn't some kind of maniac who lurked in deep water waiting for unsuspecting night swimmers. Maybe he just waited for said swimmer to return to the beach lulled into a false sense of security instead…but when she checked he was clearly heading to the far side of the beach, not even looking in her direction. As they'd agreed. Which was a good thing. And she wasn't even the teensiest bit disappointed.

It was far less pleasant pulling her dress back over her wet body than it had been to shuck it off. She'd hoped that an evening walk and swim would distract her from an ever-lengthening list of questions and worries. She stifled an unexpected giggle; to be fair her plan had worked, although in a very unexpected way. She hadn't thought about bills or her future once in the last ten minutes.

Posy took a few steps along the beach, heading for the jetty, almost hidden on one side, which led to the private path up to the villa, via the natural thermal pool. The pool might be famous but, like much of her godmother's legacy, she would gladly swap it for a roof that didn't leak in places, a new boiler and some idea of how she was going to pay the bills over the next few months whether she stayed here or not. What on earth would she do if she stayed here—and where would she go if she didn't?

Posy stopped as panic overwhelmed her, almost crushing her chest so she could barely breathe. She wrapped her arms around her torso, as if by squeezing tight she could push the terror out. Stay here or leave, she had nowhere to go, no purpose. Without dance who was she? What was she? How would she get up each day?

'Posy? Are you okay?'

It took a while before the words penetrated through the grey mist. Posy looked up to see Nico—still on his side of the arch—looking at her, concern etched on his face. She forced a deep breath, dragging the night air into her lungs. 'Yes. Thanks.'

He didn't move. 'That didn't look okay to me.'

She forced herself upright, forced her arms to loosen in a pose of defiance and strength she didn't come close to feeling. 'What happened to straight home no looking?'

His mouth quirked into a half-smile. 'I just wanted to check on you. Turns out there's all kinds of strange people lurking in this bay nowadays.'

She should go. She meant to go. Yet once again her limbs, usually so obedient, used to being kicked up high and held in gravity-defying positions, refused to move a single step. 'There are. Very chivalrous of you to think of me.'

'I'm a chivalrous type.' The sun had almost set behind him, casting a red glow over him, making him otherworldly, the cove a place of magic and mystery. He was taller than she had realised, lean to the point of slimness but with a coiled strength apparent in his stance, in the definition in his arms and legs. Casual in a grey T-shirt and khaki shorts, his dark hair, wet from the sea, falling over his eyes, he still radiated a confidence and purpose she coveted. Barely aware of what she was doing, she took a step closer and then another. He didn't move but his eyes tracked her every movement. Posy was used to feeling graceful, assured in her every gesture, but right now she didn't know what to do with her limbs, every part of her body a stranger.

She knew his name, nothing more—no, that wasn't quite true. She knew that he had craved an hour's peace and solitude. Knew that she couldn't tear her gaze away from his, knew that every fibre in her body was aching to be given a purpose, a meaning. She was a creature of movement, she belonged in the dance, in the pairings of a duet or the exhilaration of many feet and arms all placed in exactly the right way at exactly the right time. For so many years that had been enough. Or so she'd thought.

But it wasn't. Pouring her body and soul into her craft had left her lacking. She had no fire; she hadn't lived. Those overheard words had burned through her, the truth of them hurting the most.

With the sunset blazing behind him Nico looked like a fire god personified, Mars come to earth blazing. Could some of that fire touch her? Warm her? Bring her to life?

Posy took another step. He leaned against the arch, watching her every move. She swallowed, the dryness in her throat a mixture of apprehension—and anticipation. 'Not too chivalrous, I hope.'

He stilled. 'Depends on the task.'

'If I was a selkie, would you hide my seal skin, just for the night?'

'I never thought that was playing fair. I'd prefer the selkie to come to me of her own free will.'

'Would she?'

'I think so.'

Another step. He was close now, close enough that, even as the dusk drew in, Posy could see the heat in his eyes, the tension in his stance for all his supposed nonchalance, the muscle beating in his cheek. He felt it, this connection. He wanted her. 'I think so too. Just for one night.'

He nodded, understanding her every meaning. 'You can't trap a wild creature.'

Her entire life Posy had put ballet first. Her few relationships fizzling out, hardly mourned, they were so unimportant compared to her career. Bruno might feel that she lacked passion but everything she had was poured into her work. Without it she had no outlet, her emotions, her physical energy pent up, her worries needing an outlet. She'd thought a swim might help. She'd been wrong. But Nico might. If she let him.

If she let herself.

Posy Marlowe did not go skinny dipping. Posy Marlowe certainly didn't flirt with strangers in the sea, on the beach. Posy Marlowe would never tug her dress off and stand naked in front of a complete stranger as the sun dipped below the horizon, the only sound the hush of the waves on the shore. With shaking hands she clasped the fabric and tugged, letting the cotton slither onto the beach as she stood before him. His intake of breath emboldened her. 'You might tame it for an evening, though.'

'Not too tame, I hope.' He stepped away from the arch as he spoke, stepped close and looked into her face for one long moment, searching for truth, for consent, for surety. She appreciated it even as impatience surged, her hand reaching for his chest, tracing the lines of his muscles. She knew muscles, their purpose, look and feel. She'd never quite appreciated them before today as he quivered ever so slightly under her touch before capturing her hand with his even as his head bent towards hers, his mouth firm and sweet, his touch knowing and sure as he took control. Posy knew all about being led, the steps in a duet, and she sank into his kiss, into his touch, into his arms. Living. For one night only.

CHAPTER THREE

NICO BOWED SMOOTHLY in his uncle's direction before backing out of the Great Hall, working hard to keep the irritation off his face. He'd lost his temper too many times in the past and it had never got him anywhere. His uncle made a toddler in the middle of a tantrum seem reasonable, which meant rational debate was as unlikely to work as anger. When King Vincenzo V made his mind up it was well and truly up and neither logic nor reason could shift it. In the past Nico had simply circumnavigated his uncle's wishes but things were infinitely more complicated now.

'Dammit, Alessandro,' he said softly as he finally made his way out of the double doors and into the opulent hallway. 'You could always handle him so much better than me.' The guards standing smartly to attention either side of the

open doors, hot and ridiculous in the full bur-
nished splendour of their dress uniforms, didn't
betray that they had heard his words with as
much as a flicker of an eyelid. Maybe he should
take lessons from them.

The hallway was wide enough for two cars to
drive down it with ease, the vaulted ceiling at
double height, the marble floor kept so highly
polished Nico doubted it had ever been subjected
to a health and safety risk assessment. As small
boys he and Alessandro had skated along here
under the disapproving eyes of ancestors frown-
ing down from huge portraits, careering along,
narrowly missing the spindly chairs and occasional tables that were dotted along like valu-
able obstacles in their headlong race. At intervals
discreet doors were set into the ornate panelling,
leading to suites of offices, other function rooms
and rooms that Nico had discovered no discern-
ible use for. He had his own suite now, one here
for work, meetings and audiences as well as his
private rooms, in the west wing. At least they
hadn't tried to give him Alessandro's rooms yet.

It was hard enough to feel at home in the high-ceilinged formal rooms without mementoes of his cousin scattered around his living quarters.

Not that he'd ever really felt at home here. He'd spent too much time alone in the family suite while his parents had jetted off to Paris, to London, to New York and even when they'd been resident in the palace they'd barely seemed to notice he was there, too busy enjoying the luxuries and privileges of royal life to settle for anything as mundane as private family meals or playing with their son. Luckily he'd been a firm favourite of his grandmother's—and he'd idolised his cousin, two years older yet with plenty of time for his younger shadow. They were all the family he had needed. And now one was gone and the other fading fast.

'Your Highness?'

It still took a few seconds for the title to register in Nico's brain and for him to respond. In a way he hoped that never changed, that he wouldn't supplant his cousin so easily. He stopped and allowed the harried official rushing along the corridor to catch up with him.

'Your Highness.' She was breathing hard, swaying in her too-high heels. Every official dressed as if they were being judged on their power dressing skills, aggressively cut suits the unspoken palace uniform; Nico's own faded jeans and checked shirt were a pointed contrast. 'Her Grace would like to see you at your earliest convenience.'

Which meant now. Nico's grandmother, in her own way, was just as stubborn as his uncle. 'Thank you.'

The official hesitated; obviously she had orders to bring him then and there but Nico had no intention of being ordered around by anyone, not even Graziella del Castro, Dowager Queen. 'I'll be along shortly,' he added. She didn't look too placated but nodded and marched away, her heels perfectly balanced on the marble floor. Nico paused, his mini rebellion feeling as paltry as it was. It wasn't his grandmother he was angry at— nor even his uncle. It was fate. Fate for snatching away his cousin and landing him here in this unwanted spot with this unwanted future. He pivoted and caught up with the official in three long strides. 'Don't worry, I'll head there now.'

She gave him a startled look; palace officials were never worried—at least they were well trained not to look it—but nodded as Nico headed off in the direction of his grandmother's rooms.

Like her son, the King, and Nico himself his grandmother had two sets of rooms, her formal receiving and business rooms in the main part of the palace and her own private suite in the west wing, compromising her bedroom, her sitting room, dining room, study and roof terrace. Up to a year ago she would usually be found downstairs during the day, sitting erect at her desk in her office or on the ornate chair in her receiving room, refusing to slow down despite having achieved her seventieth birthday a few years before. But since Alessandro's death she tended to spend more and more time in her private rooms and it was towards these Nico headed, up the grand staircase, along the balcony that overhung the famous hall, the oldest part of the original castle, and through a discreet—at least it would have been if it weren't for the two heavily armed soldiers guarding it—door that led to the royal family's private apartments.

The door led into another corridor, as luxurious as the main hallway that bisected the palace in two, but less ornate. These rooms weren't designed to impress and, although Nico personally found the rose velvet and cream a little cloying, it was a refreshing contrast to the pomposity of the gilt and purples in the public parts of the palace. His own rooms were on the top floor but his grandmother's were on the first, and it only took a minute before he was rapping gently on her door to hear her voice bid him 'Enter'. He did as he was told, sweeping a low bow before her and taking her hand in his and raising it to his lips. 'Your Grace.'

Graziella didn't look at all impressed by his display of manners. 'Don't humbug me, young man.'

Nico rocked back on his heels and grinned unrepentantly down at her. Her silver hair was in its usual elegant chignon and she was dressed with her customary chicness but the shadows under her eyes—and the shadows *in* her eyes—were new. No wonder, she had lost her husband, youngest son and grandson in the space of five years.

His grandfather's heart attack had come as no real shock, the warning signs had been there for years, but Nico's own father's untimely death in a helicopter crash followed shortly by Alessandro's sudden collapse had rocked the family—and the island—to the core. Nico still didn't understand how a man as healthy, as strong as Alessandro could just drop down dead—and none of the reading he'd done on Sudden Arrhythmic Death Syndrome could convince him that he couldn't have done something, anything, to prevent it if only he'd known.

In that way he was still well and truly stuck in the first stage of grief—denial. He could have held several medical degrees and been right there and still he couldn't have done anything to save his cousin.

The remaining members of the family still all

suffered, still all grieved, but his grandmother had been the slowest to return to some semblance of normality. Nico tried to hide his concern as his smile widened. 'Not humbugging, just showing respect.'

'Hmm, and did you show your uncle the same degree of respect?' She waved him towards the uncomfortable-looking sofa that sat at right angles to her own chair and Nico obediently perched on the edge of the slippery satin.

'Of course. At least,' he amended, 'I refrained from calling him a fool in public.'

'Nico, he doesn't like change, you know that.'

She might closet herself away in her rooms but she still knew everything that went on in every hidden palace corner. 'Grandmamma, we have no choice. Change will come whether we like it or not. Better that we control it rather than let it control us.'

'But tourists, Nico.' His grandmother couldn't have sounded more disgusted if he'd suggested tearing down the ancient woodlands to build a nuclear power station. 'With their noise and their litter and their shorts and all they can eat. It's never been our way.'

'It depends on the tourists, Grandmamma.' He'd already made exactly these points to his uncle. Nico took a deep breath and re-embarked on the speech he'd prepared. 'We already get a few who make the journey here *because* we're unspoilt, to walk or swim or relax. We just need more of them. We won't be able to compete with the established Mediterranean resorts and nor should we, but if we market ourselves to honeymooners and couples as a luxury holiday destination and to the thrill seekers who will love our mountains and lakes then we won't need to change too much. Invest in some new hotels, enable our cafés and restaurants to cater for more people, improve our transport links. Nothing too scary, I promise.'

'But...'

'Our people need jobs. Our schools and hospitals need investment. Our youth need a reason to stay. We don't want them all heading off the island to start their lives elsewhere.'

As he had done.

'But why, Nico? You've only just come home. Why shake things up now with your consultants and plans? Give your uncle some time.'

'There is no time, Grandmamma.' He paused, unsure how much to tell her. 'Look. You know I spent the last year at Harvard doing an MBA. As part of that I studied our finances really carefully.'

The island monarchy wasn't purely constitutional and the royal family still took a very active role in government. Once Nico had begun to comprehend how much rode on his new position as heir to the throne he'd realised how ill equipped he was for such a responsibility and so had given up his research position at MIT to study business at Harvard instead. It hadn't taken him long to realise how much work he had ahead of him. A lifetime's work.

'I loved my grandfather, you know that, but he was a lavish spender, his father too. Look at how they redecorated the palace—all that marble imported in. And the rest: planes, cars, villas, ski lodges...'

'And an apartment for every mistress, an annuity for every mistress, jewellery for every mistress—and there were a lot of mistresses.' Bitterness coated his grandmother's voice for one unguarded second.

'For two generations the island was ignored in favour of jet-setting and pleasure. L'Isola dei Fiori needs a lot of careful managing to make up for fifty years of neglect.'

'And you think tourism will do that?'

'I think it's a start. We need more, some kind of real industry as well but that's a whole other step. One day I would like to see the island a beacon of innovation for renewable energy and other forms of eco-friendly engineering. Expand the university, bring in the expertise, offer the right companies, the right entrepreneurs the right deal so they settle here, build here and create jobs here.' That had always been his dream. That was why he had put in the hours at MIT, made the right contacts, had worked towards his PhD, never giving up hope that, even if he couldn't persuade his uncle to throw the weight of the government behind him, he could still return in his own time, at his own will, to start up his own research company.

But the current crisis needed a quicker fix and his own dreams had to be set aside, just as he'd set his research aside.

'Tell me how I can help, Nico.'

He patted his grandmother's hand gratefully. 'You're a key part of my strategy, Grandmamma. First of all I need you to work on my uncle. I know he's done his best to put things right but selling the odd yacht and ski lodge isn't enough. He needs to give the tourism campaign his full backing and ensure the rest of his ministers do as well.'

'What did he say today?'

'The usual. That I'm too young to understand, that I've been gone too long, that I think fancy degrees from fancy universities make up for my own lack of sense.' He grinned at her. 'Nothing he hasn't said a million times before.' It didn't stop the words from stinging though. He was thirty-two, not twenty, and he was proud of his degrees. He'd worked damn hard for them. But his uncle preferred to believe the rubbish in the papers than the evidence before him. Nico had been labelled a playboy Del Castro in his teens, like his father and grandfather before him, and his uncle had no intention of challenging that narrative.

Graziella drew herself up. 'I'll speak to him.'

'Thank you, Grandmamma. There are another couple of things. I need to marry...'

'Yes?' Her eyes lit up. This was exactly the kind of project she relished.

'And I need you to choose me a bride. I know you have a list of suitable names and that's fine. Better to find a girl who has been raised to manage this kind of life than throw some hapless innocent into the circus. I just have one request...'

'Just one?'

'I need a bride who is willing to be wooed. Publicly. The marketing consultant thinks a royal wedding is the perfect international showcase for L'Isola dei Fiori and we should milk it as much as possible. You know, boat rides into the grottos, horse rides through meadows, a royal ball...' He grinned at the revolted expression on her face.

'I had no idea you were such a romantic, Nico.'

'I'm not a romantic. I'm a realist. There's nothing people like better than a royal love story. So pick me a girl who will play her part and I'll marry her. The papers follow me around anyway. I might as well make use of my reputation.'

As a young, unattached prince he'd attracted the gossip magazines like wasps flocking around a sweet drink at the tail end of summer. If he'd lived quietly they might have left him alone eventually but he'd hung out with a young, moneyed crowd, enjoying time away from his studies at parties in New York, summer houses in the Hamptons, winter breaks in the Bahamas, on yachts, in clubs throughout Europe. At first it had been an exquisite relief, freedom after the strictures of a childhood at court. At some point it had become habit.

His grandmother nodded. 'Everyone loves a reformed playboy, I suppose. I'll find you a suitable bride. But, Nico? Just be discreet, when you find other amusements.' And for a fleeting second she looked so vulnerable Nico felt a surge of anger against the grandfather who had put that look on her face—and emptied the palace coffers to do so.

'No need. When I marry I'll be faithful. It might be arranged but that's no reason to treat marriage like it's meaningless. I hope I'm better than that.' As he said the words a fleeting image passed through his mind, a slim girl on the beach, hair tumbling around her breasts, eyes on his. He'd known then it was his last act of freedom, a sweet goodbye. Something to carry him through the years of duty that lay ahead.

'And the other thing?'

He winced. He knew she would dislike his next proposal. 'If we're going to start the campaign soon we need a few places ready for the tourists we're hoping to attract. There's a few decent city hotels, a couple of beach places and some lovely guesthouses but none of the boutique hotels that the kind of holiday makers we want to attract prefer. The consultant has suggested that we invest in several now, do them up over the winter ready for next season.'

'And?'

'And one of the places she suggested is Villa Rosa.'

His grandmother didn't answer but she drew herself up, her mouth tight. Nico watched her sympathetically. Until early last year the villa had been occupied by an aging beauty who, had been involved in a very public and very steamy affair with his grandfather, who had visited her, semi discreetly, by sailing around to the cove at night. The owner had died recently and the villa, as far as he knew, lay empty. His grandmother had always behaved with a dignified ignorance where his grandfather was concerned but installing a mistress on the island had pushed even her resilience to the limit.

'It has a certain notoriety that will draw people in: the parties that were held there, the famous people that stayed there—and of course the thermal pool and the secret beach.'

'I see.'

'I'm sorry to bring it up, Grandmamma, but I think the consultant's right. It is the perfect location and the Villa Rosa markets itself. Plus the lawyers say it's likely that my grandfather shouldn't have gifted the villa away in the first place; because it is so close to the cliff top and because it has access down to the beach it's situated on Crown land and therefore...'

'Therefore it can't be sold or owned by a private individual.'

'Or inherited,' he confirmed. He hesitated. 'I know you keep tabs on everything that goes on around here. I wondered if you know who owns it now? I could ask around but I don't want word to get out that we're interested.'

His grandmother shrugged. 'Apparently that woman left it to a niece or something but it's been empty or used as a holiday home since she died—they tell me it needs a lot of work. What are you going to do? Serve her notice?'

Nico shook his head. 'No. I'll offer her money to sell. We don't want the delay or cost of going to court—nor the publicity. But we can pay a fair price, tied up in a lot of legal documents that will hopefully persuade her to say yes sooner rather than later.

'Do you know anything about this owner? Where she's from?'

His instincts had been right. His grandmother knew everything. She tilted her chin. 'England, but I believe she arrived on the island a week ago. By public ferry, coach class, one battered bag.'

Which meant she had been there when he and Posy...an unwelcome thought hit him. He hadn't, had he? 'What's her name?'

'Marlowe. Rosalind Marlowe.'

Relief flooded through him. Not the same woman after all. And coach class with one bag? That added up to one cash-strapped English-woman. She'd be putty in his hands. The sooner he got his tourism project up and running, the sooner he got married, then the sooner he could work on his ideas and create something real, something sustainable in his homeland. And then this whole Crown Prince deal might start to feel less like an unwanted burden and more like something he could live with.

It was time to pay the owner of the Villa Rosa one very official visit.

CHAPTER FOUR

Posy crossed the courtyard and eyed the garages curiously. They were in pretty good nick, their roofs sounder than that of the house itself. They would, with new doors, a new floor, heaters and a sound system, make pretty awesome studios.

Just a quick DIY job then. Posy mentally totted up the possible costs, wincing before she got to the sprung floor, mirrors and barre. Converting wasn't going to be that much cheaper than building from scratch and right now she was more geared up for a 'lick of paint and a good clean' type budget.

Of course, she could always sell the stylish vintage car that she'd inherited along with the villa to pay for the work. Her sisters would never forgive her—she'd already had to hear rhapsodies about engines and paintwork and rpms—but unlike the rest of the Marlowes Posy's interest in transport was limited to did it work and would it get her where she needed to go? Hanging onto a vintage car for the sake of it when it could be turned into cold, hard cash would be utter folly.

Maybe she should offer Miranda and Imogen first refusal though…for a reasonable price because goodness knew she needed the money.

She pivoted and looked closely at the villa in all its faded glory, trying not to glaze over the imperfections. Thanks to Immi the gardens were looking a lot more manageable and her sisters—and their various husbands and fiancés—had all helped make the inside more home-like, but there was no way she could even consider opening to paying guests until she had fixed the roof, put in a new boiler and pulled the kitchen into the twenty-first century. Then she'd have to make sure the bathrooms were all in decent enough condition for non-family use and check each bed for broken springs or damp. She'd need bed linen as well. And she still needed actually to qualify as a Pilates and ballet teacher...

She sighed. The way she saw it she had two choices. Either she sold the villa or she stopped it being a liability and turned it into an asset. And it could, with some work—okay, a lot of work—be a very considerable asset. The island was famed for its hot springs, the rock pool offered a natural bathing experience all year round and the view and the gardens were tranquil enough to soothe any stressed city dweller. She had bedrooms to spare, more bathrooms than she could use if she bathed in a different one every day and plenty of nooks where people could settle with books or just to doze.

She had the space, she had the contacts, she had the knowledge and, if she sold the car and ransacked some of the contents of the villa, she might be able to muster up enough money.

Posy blew out a frustrated breath. Her other choice was to sell. That would solve the money problem but left her with no idea what a twenty-four-year-old ex-ballerina with one good GCSE to her name could do for the rest of her life.

And the Marlowes were famously long-lived.

Of course there was nothing stopping her jumping on a plane and returning to London either. When she'd falteringly handed in her notice Bruno had taken a far too keen look at her before telling her to keep in shape and exercise and if she changed her mind within the year there would still be a place for her in the company. For all her resolution to start again, when she lay awake in the middle of the night the prospect of slinking back and resuming her place in the Corps de Ballet was far too tempting. But if she returned to London would that make her a double failure? Prove that she didn't know how to live?

But she'd lived last night…

Heat flared in her cheeks, an answering warmth in her breasts and low deep in her stomach and she fought the urge to hide behind her hands like a small girl caught out in a misdeed. What had she been thinking? Taking her clothes off in front of a complete stranger? Allowing him—no, wanting him—to touch her like that in public? She had never behaved so recklessly, so provocatively. It was all too easy to blame the moonlight, the sea, the need to feel wanted. But she was the one who had wanted. She was the one who had initiated. Not that she'd kept that control for long...

She shivered as flashbacks of deep, sweet kisses, long, torturous caresses, whispered endearments overwhelmed her. She had never known it to be like that, at once so wild and urgent and yet so tender. It had taken every inch of resolution to walk away, disappearing before midnight because every fairy tale reader knew not to stay beyond the witching hour. They'd agreed on just the one evening but she'd taken her time as she'd moved along the beach, just in case he called after her, asked to see her again.

She'd been half disappointed when he hadn't, the feeling intensifying when she'd reached the jetty and turned back to find him gone. Okay, more than half disappointed.

Posy wandered back towards the house, the day

stretching before her, empty and meaningless just like the day before and the day before that. She'd mechanically stretched and gone through her exercises earlier that morning, keeping her muscles warm and her body supple, but her books sat unopened, her crochet hook lay unused and the colouring books were still pristine. Turned out she wasn't much good at relaxing and doing nothing.

Maybe she should start going through the house—she had a list of contents somewhere along with valuations. Whether she sold up or sold enough to convert the villa into a retreat she still needed to know what was where and if she wanted to keep any of it—not that her tastes ran to shelves filled with vases, ornaments, boxes and the numerous other knick-knacks that filled the villa. When she had come to visit her godmother as a child she'd loved to play with them all, creating intricate games and scenarios for the various china animals. Now they were just clutter, gathering dust.

The double doors that led into the grand double-height conservatory stood open, the sun reflecting off the panes of coloured glass randomly interspersed with the plain glass. It must have been gorgeous in Sofia's, her godmother's, heyday, filled with climbing plants winding their way up the leaded panes, providing much-needed shade and contrast. Sofia had held parties in the room attended by movie stars, European aristocrats and millionaires; if Posy closed her eyes she could still see the glittering jewels around the throats and in the ears of the women, the long, elegant cigarette holders, the cocktails circulating on silver trays. If rumour was to be believed Sofia had had her own share of diamonds and other precious stones but all that was left was paste and crystal, pretty but worthless. Sofia had sold them all as her looks had faded and her lovers had melted away.

She'd still been a consummate hostess though. Posy had loved coming here. Sofia had always treated Posy and her sisters as if they were small adults, not children. Posy had never known what to expect from one day to the next—they might get dressed up in some of Sofia's old couture gowns and hold a party, canapés and mocktails at three in the afternoon for just them. Or Sofia might decide they needed to redecorate the dining room, or teach them to snorkel, or take them into the town for oysters and champagne. But mostly she allowed them freedom to swim, sunbathe and run free so that they returned to the UK tanned and relaxed. Posy treasured the visits even more once she had started at ballet school, her holidays no relaxing time off but filled with residential courses around the country. The two carefree weeks she managed to snatch at Sofia's were a welcome contrast to the rigid, disciplined life she had chosen. The rigid, disciplined life she was trying so hard not to miss.

She jumped as the bell tolled solemnly. Who could that be? The house had been empty since Immi left a month ago and no one apart from her family knew she was here.

She didn't have to answer it. If she stayed quiet they would probably just go away.

The bell tolled again, low and commanding.

'Don't be such a coward,' she scolded herself. After all Imogen's fiancé, Matt, had lived on the island for several years. It would be just like Immi to get a friend of Matt's to check up on her. She knew her sisters were worried about her decision to move into her money pit of an inheritance, to leave London, to quit her hard-fought-for career; of course they'd send in an intervention.

Well, the intervention could just intervene right out. She was fine. Almost.

The bell tolled for a third time as she moved briskly through the hall, a room large enough to hold a ball in if the conservatory was otherwise engaged, and she wrenched open the front door, indignation buzzing through her veins. 'Hold your horses. I'm here. Oh!'

Her hand tightened on the door. 'Nico?'

She wasn't sure at first. The expression in the blue eyes was a mixture of surprise and determination, the dark hair slicked back, the broad shoulders and narrow waist covered by a perfectly cut light suit. But her body knew him instantly, every pulse beating rapidly as he looked straight at her.

'Hello, Posy.'

Any thought he might have come looking for her, that this was the start of the kind of whirlwind romance she'd read about but never experienced, evaporated in the late morning sun. There was no flirtatiousness in his voice, no seduction in his eyes. Whatever Nico wanted here it didn't include a re-enactment of last night.

That was fine. She didn't expect anything else. Hoped maybe, in that first flare of surprise, that he might be pleased to see her but two could play at the 'polite strangers' game. She forced her hand to relax, her face to remain still, her highly trained muscles obeying in instant precision. 'How can I help?'

'I'm looking for Rosalind Marlowe. Is she here?'

'You're talking to her. I'm Rosalind,' she clarified as his forehead crinkled. 'Rosalind shortened to Rosy, my family called me Rosy-Posy and then when I started to dance, they kind of

lost the Rosy in a *Ballet Shoes* Posy Fossil way.'
She was babbling. Great. 'Not that that matters.
What do you want?'

The mask had slipped a little; Nico was looking uncomfortable. 'Can I come in?'

'I don't know,' she said honestly. 'I didn't expect to see you again after last night and now
here you are looking for me but not knowing it's
me. I don't want someone who makes me uncomfortable in my house. So probably not. Whatever
you want to say to me you can say right here.'

Nico narrowed his eyes. Two minutes in and already this whole situation was slipping dangerously out of control. It was his own fault. He
should have heeded the warning bells clanging
loudly the instant his grandmother mentioned
that the villa had passed to an Englishwoman.
There was a reason Posy had sprung straight into
his mind. She was the logical choice, appearing
on the beach the way she had last night, her con-
viction that he was trespassing, her surety that
she was safe to swim naked—but the difference

in name had allowed him to ignore his premonition. Big mistake.

None of this would matter if he hadn't given in to temptation last night; this was a lesson, if ever he needed one, not to engage in *al fresco* fun and games with complete strangers. Maybe it was a good thing he was about to be safely and dutifully married.

Posy held onto the heavy oak door as if it were supporting her—and as if any moment she might swing it shut in his face. Nico suppressed a smile—he couldn't remember anyone refusing him entry before.

She was casually dressed in soft grey yoga trousers and a matching vest top, her gorgeous dark hair twisted up into a messy bun, her face make-up free, emphasising the disparity between them. He'd wanted to wrong-foot Rosalind Marlowe, to impress her with his title, his designer suit, his offer. He didn't want to wrong-foot Posy, dark-eyed naiad of the night before. He should have called first, given her a chance to put her armour on just as he had his.

Either way he needed a sharp change of tactic. 'In that case will you take a short walk with me? Just along the cliff top,' he added as she stared at him doubtfully. 'There's a matter I really need to discuss with you.'

'Is it to do with last night?' Pink blossomed on her cheeks as she asked the question but she held his gaze defiantly.

'Last night? No. I didn't realise you lived here.'

'Where did you think I lived? There's no other house for a mile.'

'Secretly I thought you really had come from the sea—or more prosaically that you'd sailed round. Not many people think they're allowed to stop off at the beach but those who do know that they're almost guaranteed to have the beach to themselves and that the jetty makes it a safe mooring.'

'We always assumed it belonged to the Villa Rosa. The beach, I mean. We never saw anyone else on it when we were kids. It was our own playground.'

'We?'

'My sisters and I. There's four of us.'

'Four? Are any of them here with you now?'

'They've all been and gone. The villa's been a bit of a godsend this year. I don't know what we'd have done without it. I didn't expect Sofia—my godmother—to leave it to me and I'm not entirely sure what to do with it but I'm grateful we all had somewhere to come when we needed it.'

She wasn't entirely sure what to do with it— there, that was positive. Better focus on that than the glow in her eyes when she had mentioned how grateful she was to own it.

'Look, Nico, we can't keep talking like this. Come on in. I didn't mean to be rude but you startled me.'

She held the door open and Nico stepped into the large, light-filled hallway. The panelling was painted white and hung with bright abstract paintings, the floor covered in white tiles; a glass-sided staircase curved along one wall onto the landing above. Doors on either side stood ajar; through one he glimpsed a huge dining table capable of seating at least twenty, through another a room filled with vintage furniture, the plastered walls covered in delicate murals. But for all its sumptuousness the famed Villa Rosa felt shabby and a little grubby, cobwebs coating the plasterwork, lines of grime in between the tiles.

'I know, it's kind of ridiculous for one person, isn't it? Far too much to look after.' Posy read his thoughts with unerring accuracy. 'Of course, when she first lived here, Sofia—my godmother—filled the place with visitors. She didn't really live on her own until the mid-eighties. And it must have been so expensive to keep up—some rooms are just covered in dust sheets and shut away. This way. Do you want a drink?'

'No. Thank you.'

Nico's eyes widened as she took him through another faded, but lavishly decorated and ornamented, hallway and into an impressive, if in need of urgent repair, conservatory. He was right. This place would make a superb boutique hotel.

It was also disconcerting. His grandfather's influence was stamped all over the place, in the hunting prints hung along one wall to the cushions flung casually on a wooden bench, embroidered with King Ludano's own personal seal. The parties held here were legendary—parties his grandfather had funded and attended rather than concentrating on improving the lives of the people who lived and worked on the island that gave him his title and their loyalty.

Nico rocked back on his heels and stared up at the roof. He'd been so busy mourning the loss of the future he had been working towards, so busy mourning his cousin, so busy bitterly resenting the title and responsibilities due his way that he'd forgotten what it all meant. Forgotten what he owed every man, woman and child born on this island or who chose to make their home here. A monarchy might be absurdly old-fashioned but that was what they had and it was up to him to make the best of it.

Duty, honour, service.

He turned and smiled at Posy, pushing his sympathy for her to one side. 'I'm afraid there's a problem with the villa. It doesn't look like your godmother was entitled to leave it to you after all.'

* * *

Duty, honour, service. They might be worthy but they weren't particularly nice. The memory of the stricken look in Posy's eyes when he'd explained the situation to her was very hard to shake—and even the very generous under the circumstances settlement he'd mentioned hadn't lifted her spirits.

'I can't think. I need to, I need to talk to someone,' she'd said, clutching the deeds and official settlement in her hands. 'I'll be in touch. You have to give me time—unless you're planning to throw me out straight away?'

He'd reassured her that she had all the time she needed—within reason. 'But we do need an answer fast. The settlement offered is dependent on a swift, uncontested acceptance,' he'd warned her and walked away, leaving her standing alone in the vast conservatory, the papers twisted in her hands.

He had only just returned to the castle when he saw the same, harried-looking aide waiting for him, still teetering on the same uncomfortable heels, heels matched by the look on her face. She didn't want to summon him as much as he didn't want to be summoned. 'Sir, Your Highness...'

Nico supplied the rest. 'My grandmother?'

'Yes, if you would be so kind. She said it was of the utmost importance.'

'Then it would be rude to keep her waiting. Thank you.'

She managed a quick smile of relief before rushing away on whatever other errand his grandmother had devised. Nico paused. He really didn't want to discuss Posy with his grandmother and she probably wanted to see him to elicit more information about the new owner of the villa. He needed a deflection and what better way to deflect a doting grandmother than with a potential bride? She'd sent him away with a terrifyingly thorough dossier on some of Europe's most eligible young women for him to shortlist candidates from. Perfect.

Ten minutes later and armed with his grandmother's dossier, Nico tapped on her door once again. He expected the usual faint murmur and to let himself into the room. Instead the door was flung open and his grandmother stood there, eyes blazing and her usually pale cheeks flushed. 'It's unfortunate that you take after your grandfather in looks, but to take after him in actions too? Are you planning to bankrupt what's left of the island's economy while you're at it?'

Nico's lips tightened. 'Nice to see you as well, Grandmother, especially on your feet and so animated. Do you mind if I can come in so we can have this interesting discussion in private or would you like us to invite the TV station in and broadcast live to the nation, not just to the palace?' He kept his voice as normal as possible but his grandmother took a chastened step backwards, leaving the way clear for him to walk into her room, closing the door firmly behind him as he did so.

She wasn't alone. Her private secretary was perched on the sofa, hands clasped and mouth pursed disapprovingly. Nico nodded in her direction. There was clearly not much point in turning on the famous charm. To his surprise Anna, the marketing consultant, was also sitting down; a tablet and a laptop lay on the table in front of her. She could barely meet his eye. What was going on? Had his uncle interfered already and shut down his plans?

'It's a little late to worry about broadcasting to the nation, Nico,' his grandmother said peevishly. 'After everything you said this morning as well.'

Nico stared. 'Would you mind just explaining what's going on here?'

Anna picked up the tablet and handed it over, still without meeting his eye or saying a word. Nico took it and touched the screen to bring it to life. He blinked. 'What the hell?'

'That's not the worst of it.' His grandmother sniffed. 'Not all of them are pixelated.'

'What?' He stared at the screen in utter disbelief.

Splash! screamed the headline. *Prince Nico and mystery brunette steaming up the sea!*

Somehow the photographer had zoomed in to show Nico in the water facing Posy, their shoulders naked, the look on his face unmistakable. Lust. Interest. Desire. 'Dammit.'

'It gets worse,' his grandmother said, snatching the tablet from him and swiping. She wasn't exaggerating. Shots of them kissing on the beach, just a few pixels concealing their nudity. Then today, Posy at the door of the villa, her face set, watching him walk away. *Lovers' tiff?* the shot was captioned.

Nico turned away in disgust.

'Ghouls.'

'Yes—and you fed them,' his grandmother retorted. 'What were you thinking? No, don't answer that. You clearly weren't thinking. Who is she, Nico? Is she related to that woman?'

'Not exactly. She is her goddaughter, though, and the current owner of the Villa Rosa. Look, Grandmother. This was last night, I had no idea who she was...' He stopped. He wasn't sure his explanation was making the situation any better.

'It's not so much *who* as *where*,' his grandmother said tartly. 'In the sea? On the beach. Where anyone can see?'

Despite himself Nico's mouth curved as he remembered the first sight of Posy on the beach, the unselfconscious way she'd danced, the smooth lines of her lithe body. He should be sorry but he couldn't quite bring himself to regret much of the night before. 'You said yourself everyone loves a reformed playboy,' he said with a shrug. 'You know how deserted it is up there. I didn't see anyone when I arrived and, yes, I did check before deciding to go for a swim. It's unfortunate and a gross invasion of what little privacy I have left but it'll soon be forgotten.'

Anna stood up, her mouth tense. 'Nico, you're supposed to be wooing your bride over the next few months.'

His grandmother nodded. 'What will people think when they see you strolling hand in hand on a beach with your intended? They'll be wondering if you went skinny dipping and then rolled around in the sand, that's what they'll think. You said that we were supposed to be selling the island as a romantic destination, not an eighteen to thirties resort! Romance, Nico, not sex.'

'The two aren't mutually exclusive.' He couldn't help himself.

'Nico!'

Anna shifted her feet. 'I'm sorry, Your Majesty, but I agree with His Royal Highness.'

Nico turned to his grandmother. 'See, Grandmamma, nothing to worry about. This will soon be yesterday's news.' His thoughts flew to Posy, her defeated look as he'd walked away. She was all alone in that villa, no one else around. Vulnerable.

Anna interrupted his thoughts. 'I'm sorry, I agree that romance and sex are not mutually exclusive, not that this will be quickly forgotten and I don't think hastily bringing one of the other girls to the island and rushing into a relationship will serve as enough of a distraction. But if we could supersede these images with a whole host of positive others we control then we might be able to relegate them to a footnote.'

Nico searched through the jargon to come up with a translation. New images? 'What kind of others?'

'What kind of girl is she?'

Nico stared, bewildered. 'Posy? In what way?'

'Parents, money, lineage, education, history?'

'I don't know. We met last night, in the sea. We didn't get round to swapping business cards.'

'I'll find out because right now she's our best hope of turning this fiasco into a positive story, of taking back control and selling you, the island and this relationship as one positive package.'

'What do you mean?' his grandmother asked.

'This wasn't a one-night stand, it was an expression of love. Nico and this girl—Posy did you say her name was?—have been dating secretly for months but he didn't want to impose the rigidity of a royal relationship on her. But their love was too strong and she has come to the island to see how their relationship works in the public eye. Last night was supposed to be the last privacy you had before presenting her to your family, the island and therefore the world's media. This way we can still play out the love story as we intended and salvage this situation.'

His grandmother sat down, her face pale. 'That woman's heir? In my house?'

'That's part of the reason they had to keep the relationship secret. A Romeo and Juliet scenario. They knew you wouldn't accept Posy.' Anna sniffed. 'That will never do. Does she have a middle name?'

'She's actually Rosalind. Posy is a nickname.' Nico's mind was racing. He had to get engaged to someone after all. At least he and Posy had attraction working for them. And, much as he usually laughed at his playboy image, these pictures had shaken him, the way the captions turned something beautiful into something sordid. A rush of protectiveness overwhelmed him—he was used to the media spotlight but Posy was an innocent. How would she manage when she was doorstepped and papped every time she set foot outside? How would she cope when every future friend or date had potentially seen such an intimate side of her? He couldn't turn back the clock but he could make amends. He had accepted his life was now full of duty; he would start here and now. 'Do you think this would work?'

His grandmother grabbed his hand and the weakness of her clasp alarmed him. The righteous anger had disappeared and with it her sudden return to health. 'Are you seriously considering this, Nico?'

He patted her hand, the bones fragile beneath his palm. 'I don't know,' he said slowly. 'I need a convincing love story and if she agrees then this could be just what we're looking for. If we play out an engagement over the next few months then these pictures will hopefully be forgotten, the tourism campaign ready to roll…'

'Culminating in a royal wedding in the spring,' Anna said enthusiastically.

His grandmother paled. 'The thought of a relative of that woman…'

'She's not a relative, not as far as I know. And the Romeo and Juliet idea could be powerful, you know. Drawn together but knew it couldn't work because of family history. Let's find out as much about Posy Marlowe as possible and we can convene later and make a final decision then. But if we are going to try and change the direction of this story we need to move fast. Time is running out.'

And either way he needed to get back to the villa and get Posy out of there. He knew what it was like to be in the eye of a media storm and this one was definitely a Category Four.

CHAPTER FIVE

ONE OF THE things Posy loved best about the villa was its isolation. The sole building in the beautiful national park, it was a complete contrast to her home in London. There she shared a tiny flat with two other dancers, living in a building crammed with studios and small flats, the paper-thin walls ensuring intimacy with all her neighbours. She stepped straight outside onto a grey pavement flanking a busy main road and walked through streets thronged with people to the tourist Mecca of Covent Garden. She was surrounded by noise and bustle and humanity twenty-four hours a day, the chorus of shouts, chatter, traffic, car alarms, sirens and music so consistent she barely heard it at all.

Here she looked out across the sea on one side, the other had a view of distant mountains rising from the flower-filled meadows. The nearest village was at the edge of the park, a twenty-minute walk if she needed bread, milk or help but otherwise she was all alone, the waves crashing on the rocky shore below and the plaintive cries of the gulls the only sounds. There was no Internet, mobile signal was so patchy as to be non-existent and although the old-fashioned dial phone with its long curly cord still lived in the kitchen it had been discontinued years ago. The first few days she was here she'd liked that she was cut off from everyone and everything, that she couldn't see her fellow dancers' social media accounts full of excited chatter about classes and costumes and industry gossip.

But today she couldn't help being horribly aware of just how isolated she was. Just how alone she was.

Posy picked up the document Nico had left and read it through for what must have been the fortieth time, but the dense legalese still made no sense. The document was in English, not the Italian spoken by most islanders, but it could have been written in Elvish for all the sense it made. Nico might be pushing for a quick decision and the money he'd mentioned dependent on her just walking away but, unworldly as her sisters called her, she wasn't a total fool. She knew she needed advice. 'You were always planning to sell anyway,' she murmured. But that had been before. When she had a career that left her with no time to look after a villa a plane and ferry ride away. Now she had nothing *except* the villa she was suddenly loath to let it go.

But even if she had some means of contacting the outside world who could she ask? All her friends were dancers, and her parents had only recently returned from a year travelling the world and were now fully occupied in their aviation business. And much as she loved them Posy had never run to them with her problems. It wasn't that they wouldn't have listened or cared—it was more she didn't trust them to understand. Because as supportive as they had been of her dancing career, as proud as they were of her, her father still didn't know a *pas de chat* from a *chasse* and her mother worried more about Posy's lack of a love life than she did her lack of career progression.

As for her sisters, Miranda was pregnant and Not to Be Worried, Miranda's twin, Immi, had decided to emulate her parents and was also travelling with her new fiancé, Matt, and their eldest sister Portia was blissfully, disgustingly loved up with the gorgeous actor Javier Russo. And she was happy for them all. Goodness knew they deserved some good luck and love. It just made her even more alone, more apart from the family than usual.

She scowled at the document as if it was responsible for all her troubles—which in a way it was.

'Mrs Eveslade!' Posy dropped the paper on the table in her excitement. How could she forget? She had a lawyer. Well, Sofia had had a solicitor who had taken care of all the probate and other legalese to do with Sofia's will. Mostly she had sent Posy piles of paper Posy hadn't got round to reading, a terrifying bill that was thankfully

settled from the estate, tax documents and probate certificates and lots of other paperwork all
piled up in a shoebox in the bedroom still called
hers at her parents' house.

But one of things she remembered was the val-
uation and all the work associated with that. It
had taken months before the villa was put into
her name and she was sure that part of the delay
had been because the solicitor had been estab-
lishing ownership and land boundaries and other
things that she really should have paid more attention to. But, she distinctly remembered the solicitor saying how important it was to make sure
it was all done properly, as if Posy had intended
to sell it was better to make sure everything was
in order at the outset. So if there was any discrep-
ancy in land ownership or entitlement surely that
should have been highlighted then?

Either way she needed someone with more
qualifications than a D in GCSE maths to double check Nico's claim. She might decide to take
the money and walk away or she might not, but
she wasn't going to be bullied into anything. Of

course, that meant calling Mrs Eveslade, which wasn't the easiest of propositions. Either she walked into the village and hoped that if she fed enough coins into the antiquated phone box she might manage an international call or she could charge up her phone and walk along the cliff top until she hit a sweet spot.

She barely had any coins and she was pretty sure the island phone boxes didn't accept anything as modern as credit cards. Sweet spot it was. If only the darn spot would stay in one place and not keep moving around like a restless spirit.

Half an hour later, phone charged, Posy left the house by the small gate at the very back of the house. Hidden by a riot of clambering plants, it wasn't an obvious way in—which was probably the point. Sofia's royal lover had installed several discreet entrances into the villa although the whole island and European media had known exactly what their relationship was. This door made it easy to slip away onto the coastal path and take the back way to the village or to the jetty without being seen. Or in Posy's case it simply meant a scenic walk straight along the cliff path rather than tramping down the hot dusty road. Plus it was easier to lock the back door rather than wrestle with the imposing front door locks.

It didn't take long to skirt around the back of the house and join the cliff path on the other side, leading away from the village straight along the cliff tops and into the heart of the beautiful national park. The park was full of paths and trails perfect for hikers and climbers but Posy had seen very few during her stay and, although she appreciated the tranquillity, she couldn't help but think it a shame that the island didn't attract more tourists. It was so hospitable, the food wonderful and the climate sublime, to say nothing of the breathtaking scenery. It was just a little too off the beaten track to appeal to the masses— which was no doubt a good thing—but there was a happy medium between a trickle and a deluge and she knew plenty of adrenaline junkies who would have adored scaling the mountainous peaks towering in the distance or cycling up the foothills at top speed or walkers who would love the trails and paths.

She switched her phone on and left it to power up as she walked slowly along the path. Below the waves purred rather than roared but summer was fast approaching its end and she knew the island in autumn and winter was a less forgiving place than the dreamy, sun-drenched summer idyll. Even if the villa was hers, did she really want to stay on year round? She turned, looking out over the green plains dotted with brightly coloured flowers and low trees leading inexorably to the craggy mountains, and breathed in air untinged by car fumes, cigarettes or cooking smells. There were worse places to be.

The problem was all this choice. Posy had never had a choice before—she'd had a compulsion. From that first baby ballet class she had been on a path with only one destination and no deviations. School had been an unwelcome distraction until finally she had worn her parents down and they had agreed to allow her to audition for ballet school. Her mother had admitted later they knew how hard it was to get a place; they hadn't really considered what they would do if Posy got in. But she *had* got in and she'd stayed in despite some major culls as she'd progressed through the school. On to upper school, into the company—and there her path had halted. Leaving was the first major decision she had made since she was eleven.

And she still wasn't sure she'd done the right thing. It wasn't that she missed dance. That didn't even begin to convey how it was not having ballet in her life. She ached with loss, was sluggish with lack of purpose, empty without the daily discipline and routine. Would travelling or setting up a studio fill that emptiness? She doubted it. Maybe she should settle for technically perfect and no solos. A future as the head of the corps. There were worse things. Maybe that was growing up, accepting your limitations.

With relief she saw the bars on the top of her phone flicker into a faint life. She still had the solicitor's number and, thanks to the time difference, it could only be early afternoon in London. She'd make the call and then at least she would have done something decisive before heading back to curl up in the small snug where she ensconced herself of an evening to watch Cary Grant films on Sofia's ancient VHS player. It was *An Affair to Remember* tonight. Maybe not, with her own too brief affair all too memorable for all the wrong reasons.

With purpose she angled the phone away from the sun, ready to scroll through her contacts until she found the solicitor's number, only to stop and stare as her missed call alerts began to flash incessantly. Unknown numbers, her mother's mobile, all three of her sisters, friends, more unknown numbers. Her voicemail alert was also going crazy. What was going on? An accident? Had the baby come early? She frantically counted back. No, it was far too early. Please no. Her fingers stumbled as she struggled to retrieve her voicemail and her mobile fell to the ground; she bent to retrieve it, uncharacteristically clumsy in her haste, stumbling as she stooped.

'I wouldn't listen to that if I were you.'

Posy started at the voice, falling back onto her bottom, hardly aware of the stones digging into her tender flesh as she pushed herself back up into a sitting position. Clasping her errant phone in one hand, she glared up at the smiling Nico. How did he manage to be in the wrong place at the wrong time every time? Begrudgingly she took the hand he held out to her and allowed him to pull her up.

'Where did you come from?'

'The path. I saw you leave the villa and followed you.'

She should have been annoyed, or even scared at his words but she wasn't. Nico wasn't the charming tease or the sweet seducer of the night before, nor was he the serious suit of earlier that day. Instead he seemed thoughtful, a determined set to his shoulders as he took the phone from her hand.

'That's mine. Give it back.'

'In a minute. I need to tell you something—ask you something first.'

She made a grab for it, fear filling her, not because she was alone with a near stranger and with no way of getting help—but because of the odd look on his face. A sixth sense whispered to her that his odd behaviour was all mixed in with the missed phone calls and a dim part of her knew that somewhere, somehow, everything had changed. 'No. I have to call my sisters. Something's happened and I don't know what. Give it to me.'

But he held the phone just out of reach, compassion in the dark blue eyes. 'In a minute. Posy. Listen to me. I know what's happened.'

His calm words hit her and her hand dropped unsteadily to her side, tension competing with fear. 'You know, but how? How would they know to call you? I don't even know I know you so how would they?'

He closed his eyes briefly. 'Posy, listen to me. I haven't been entirely honest with you.'

A snort of disbelief escaped her. 'Haven't been entirely honest? Which part exactly? When you seduced me on the beach or when you marched up to my front door and told me I'm not entitled to my home? Is this all some part of an elaborate plot to what? Con me out of the villa? What kind of lawyer are you exactly?' She knew she was babbling again, but it was easier to allow the words to bubble out than hear whatever it was he had to say, find out just why the world, his wife and their cat were so desperately trying to get hold of her.

Nico held up a hand and she came to an abrupt stop, the words drying up in her mouth, and she stared at him. 'Listen to me, Posy. This is important. I'm not a lawyer. I don't represent the royal family, the Del Castros. I *am* one. I'm Nicolas Del Castro.'

'Nicolas Del Castro?'

She knew that name. How did she know it? 'You're a member of the royal family? Like, a prince or a duke or a…' She paused. What else were royals? Kings, of course, but she'd seen a picture of the current king and she couldn't remember him being drop-your-clothes-in-the-sand hot. Or indeed hot at all.

His mouth tightened. 'A prince? Yes. The Crown Prince.'

'The Crown Prince?' She stared at him, no doubt looking as stupid as she felt. 'But yesterday, today…'

'That's why I am here. Look, we were seen. Last night. That's what everyone is trying to tell you.'

Posy blinked as the world swirled to a nauseous stop and she swayed. 'Seen? When? Who by?' But she knew the answers. It was all too clear. Her phone was red hot and he was a prince—a crown prince. The answer was unlikely to be a shepherd minding his own business who'd decided to ignore the whole proceedings.

Nico's answer confirmed her thoughts. 'A photographer.'

'And it's all over the Internet, isn't it? How bad is it?'

'It's pretty explicit.'

Posy swallowed, a laugh trying to inappropriately bubble up. She'd wanted some direction, something to change. *Careful what you wish for, Posy.*

'Why are you here, Nico?'

'To bring you to the palace until we get this situation under control.'

She wanted to stamp her foot at his calmness. 'Under control? What do you mean?'

He looked at her, his face unreadable. 'I think we should get married. Don't you?'

CHAPTER SIX

POSY BLINKED, THEN blinked again. Yep, he was still here, still with that determined set to his shoulders and the same shuttered look on his face. 'You think we should what?'

'Get married.'

This was a joke, right? But there was no hint of amusement in his hard eyes.

'But…that's ridiculous. We don't even know each other.' Plus he hadn't even asked her. Not that a ring and a bended knee would make any difference but at least she wouldn't feel like a problem he needed to sort out. She folded her arms and glared at him.

Nico raised one lazy brow. 'Rosalind Anne Marlowe,' he drawled. 'Twenty-four years old. Your parents own a well-thought-of light aircraft manufacturer. You have three sisters, one a pilot, another a celebrity journalist who is married to Javier Russo, a friend of my cousin, Alessandro's.'

'Yes, but...'

He carried on as if she hadn't spoken. 'You went to train to be a ballerina when you were eleven and graduated into the Company where you spent the last five years as a member of the Corps de Ballet until your unexpected sabbatical this summer. No one knows if you plan to return to dancing or if you have other plans but your sabbatical has caused quite a stir—you have shown no interest in anything except ballet your entire life. You share a flat with two other dancers, have had a handful of boyfriends although no relationship lasted more than three months and you met them all through work. How am I doing so far?'

'That,' Posy said, trying not to shudder at the bald facts of her life laid out before her, 'is worse than a naked picture. You had me investigated?'

'Of course. The future Crown Princess of L'Isola dei Fiori can't have any skeletons in her closet and your closet is squeaky clean. Not as much as a knucklebone.'

Twenty-four and squeaky clean. No wonder she'd been dismissed as having no fire, no life. 'So you know where I went to school? Big deal. My parents' job? So what? That doesn't mean you know anything about me. You don't know my favourite book or colour or food or film...'

His eyes darkened and he took a step nearer. 'I know you like to dance on the beach even when there's no audience there to see you. I know you like the feel of cold, salt water on your bare skin and the barer the skin, the better. I know the look on your face when you make your mind up to do something and the way your hands clench when you're nervous. I know the look on your face when I touch you. I know the way you sigh, the way you moan...'

She put a hand up, warding him off, telling herself that his words were meaningless, that they weren't sinking into her, swirling through her veins. 'That's not what I meant and you know it. My sisters have all fallen in love this year and that's wonderful but I didn't feel jealous of what they have. I *don't* feel jealous. Marriage has never been my goal. Why would I marry you? Why would I marry anyone?'

'What are your plans, Posy?'

She gaped, thrown by the sudden change of subject. 'What?'

'When you leave here. Once you've escaped the paparazzi who will very soon be at your door—if they're not already—when you've got off the island and away, where will you go? Back to London?'

'I don't know. I'm on a sabbatical, remember? I'm trying to figure things out.'

'I'm offering you a job for life. It has its perks: a nice salary, a home—several homes—good holidays. You'll have to work, that's the bit the fairy tales leave out. It's not all balls and white chargers. There's a lot of opening things and state occasions and smiling while your feet hurt but as a ballerina I think you're more than qualified.'

That last bit was true; she was an expert at

smiling through sore feet. 'A job for life. How romantic.'

She turned and began to walk back to the villa. There was some of Sofia's sherry in the kitchen and if that wasn't strong enough she was pretty sure there was a dusty bottle of absinthe in one of the covered rooms. It couldn't make her hallucinate more than she clearly already was.

'There's no room for romance in my life,' Nico said soberly as he fell into step beside her. Despite all the craziness of the last few minutes Posy couldn't help but be aware of his height, of the warmth of his arm as the path pushed them together, of the way she felt his every move, his every look deep inside, the tension in her stomach, in her thighs, at his proximity. 'Look what happened when I took a chance on a night's adventure. Everything I do, everywhere I go I am scrutinised and any woman unlucky enough to be linked to me goes under the same intense spotlight. Men like me marry women who know the score. Women prepared for this world.'

An unwanted flicker of sympathy warmed her

momentarily. It sounded lonely. Almost as lonely as a loveless marriage full of duty. 'Why me? Why now? And no, don't give me the photo story. It's embarrassing, sure. But.' She flicked him a sidelong glance. 'Men usually get away with this kind of thing much easier than women. I don't think this is going to make a huge impact on your life—just make sure the next viral photograph shows you being adorable with a puppy and the world will be at your feet.' She swallowed as the impact of her words sank in, heaviness descending, blanketing and choking. There was no way she could get back on stage in the foreseeable future, knowing that everyone would be whispering, speculating, knowing...what reputable company would want someone so notorious?

'Maybe, maybe not. You're not no one. You're the goddaughter of my grandfather's mistress. We were photographed on the beach they used to throw parties on. Pictured standing outside the villa he gave her. That makes you a story, makes us a story and I think it'll take more than puppies to change this narrative. Look, Posy. I know this seems drastic but you've lived a life of discipline, I don't think life as a royal would be as chafing for you as it would for many other women, the way we have to live, the lack of privacy and freedom.'

Posy swallowed. 'You're serious. You actually think this is a real, viable option? I'm on a sabbatical, but that doesn't mean I'm ready to give up my dreams for good. I'm a dancer, not a princess. Yes, I can stand for long periods of time and curtsey in heels but even if I was crazy enough to consider agreeing—which I'm not—there's got to be more to being a princess than that.'

'Posy, I'm just trying to find a way out of this mess that works for both of us. Either you go down in history as the dancer who romped naked with the Prince or you can be a princess. Your choice.'

Posy shivered despite the balmy afternoon sun. Ballet dancers were for the most part free from the downsides of fame, their private lives unknown to the outside world. But her sister Portia was an entertainment journalist and Posy had seen how easy it was for her to tear people down, people who were famous for much more laudable reasons than a fling with a prince. She'd seen how Javier spent his life as a headline, the truth an incidental compared to the possible scandal. 'I don't want to be famous,' she half whispered. 'Or notorious. Yes, I want to be loved and admired for my dancing but once the spotlights dim I don't need or crave attention.'

'Then this has got to be hard for you but you don't have time to dwell on it. You need to decide now.'

'What's in it for you? If I say yes?' She couldn't believe she was even asking the question, asking any questions instead of marching back to the villa, packing her bags and hightailing it away from the villa and away from Nico. But hadn't she run away from obstacles just a week ago? Look how that had panned out.

'What do you mean?'

Oh, that blank look wasn't fooling her. 'I agree and I get a job for life, as you so romantically put it. I get a PR team doing their best to make sure those photos are forgotten and buried. But what about you? What do you get out of it apart from a loveless marriage?'

There was no answer for a long minute and when he did speak his voice was toneless. 'My cousin died unexpectedly the year before last. He was supposed to be the Crown Prince, the next King.'

Of course. How could she have forgotten? 'I heard, I'm so sorry.'

'Thank you. He was raised to it, to duty and country first. As the spare, a cousin at that, expectations weren't so high for me and I may have taken advantage of that.'

'May?'

For the first time that day his mouth quirked into a smile and Posy felt an answering pull. Prince or not, she doubted many people turned Nico down when he smiled in that particular way, charm mixed with devilry and a certain *aw, shucks* frankness. 'That was the narrative. Alessandro was the obedient heir and I was the wastrel always getting him into trouble. Truth was Alessandro loved trouble as much as any boy, but he loved his country more and he knew his duty. I didn't expect to be standing here, heir to an old-fashioned constitution and a dependent country, but here I am—and I love my country too. L'Isola dei Fiori needs a stable succession. It needs an heir settled down with a wife and children, the one thing Alessandro failed to do. If he had…' the smile intensified '…you and I would be having a very different discussion right now.'

Posy wasn't sure if the jolt in her stomach was in answer to that wolfish smile or the casual mention of a wife and children. That was what he'd meant by duty, wasn't it? Not just making pretty speeches and cutting ribbons but bearing his children, future princes and princesses. The begetting of those future princes and princesses. Surely, *surely* this had to be some kind of joke…

But although Nico was smiling there was still little humour in his face. She shivered, pulling her battered mind back to the matter at hand, utterly ludicrous as this whole conversation was.

'But he didn't marry and so you need a wife. Any wife.'

'That's about it. Apart from the any wife part. My grandmother went to a lot of trouble to put a shortlist aside for me.'

'I'm guessing I wasn't at the top of that list.'

'It's doubtful but you've been catapulted right up there. It seems,' he clarified, 'that recent events make it hard for me to court any of these eligible young ladies in an approved fashion.'

'Oh.' She chewed on her lip, a habit she'd thought had been trained out of her along with slouching and bad turnout. 'You don't sound too heartbroken.'

He shrugged. 'I haven't even looked at the list. I got...sidetracked.'

Her toes curled at the dark meaning in his voice. It was a good thing she wasn't even entertaining this crazy idea because Nico Del Castro was definitely a bigger bite than she could comfortably chew.

'So you pick a wife, she agrees gratefully and bang, happy ever after?'

'Not quite. Before we get married there is a nice, public falling-in-love period to go through. What do you think, Posy? Ready to be wooed and wed?'

It stood to reason that nothing about this process was going to go smoothly and, by the pursed pinch of her lips and the cloud on her brow, his intended bride was the biggest obstacle of them all. She hadn't spoken one more word since Nico had brought up the whole public wooing part of the plan. To be honest he couldn't really blame her—he had agreed to the idea but it was still far too sickly for him to easily stomach.

But the more he considered it, the more he was convinced Posy could be the right candidate for the royal role. She had poise and dignity, which were always assets, she didn't want to be Queen, which meant she had no expectations ready to be dashed, often a danger with a royal bride, and she came with no baggage. She didn't have a title or a fortune to bring to the table, no scheming relatives or concession-demanding lawyers, just a

Cinderella stroke Juliet stroke Goose Girl vibe, which had the marketing consultant salivating into her forecast spreadsheets.

So all he needed to do was convince the lady herself. She had to have an Achilles heel; he just needed to probe until he found it.

'Why ballet?'

She darted a surprised look up at him. 'What?'

'Why did you want to be a ballet dancer? The tutus?'

'How old do you think I am? Three?' Her face relaxed into a soft smile. 'Maybe a little bit the tutus, at the beginning. No, it was Sofia. She was my grandmother's best friend. They met at boarding school and, even though they lived such different lives, were such complete opposites, they were fast friends. She was like an aunt to my mother—an indulgent, impulsive, glamorous aunt—and Mum wanted to let her know she was part of the family and asked her to be my godmother. She said, Sofia, that a godmother's purpose was to spoil the child and so she did. She took me to London every Christmas for a matinee and afternoon tea at Fortnum's.' Her smile widened. 'My sisters were so jealous. It's not easy being the youngest. They all did their best to squash me so I did rather boast about my good luck.'

'And Sofia encouraged you to dance?'

'She took me to my first ballet. The Nutcracker. I was only five—Royal Opera House, a box, expensive chocolates. My mother was really doubtful I'd sit still for that long. I was rather an energetic small child, never still if I could move, but as soon as I saw the lights and the stage and the seats filled with people all dressed up and expectant I was hooked. And then the music started...' Her voice died away, her huge dark eyes glistening before she resolutely wiped a tear away. 'That was it. I wanted to be Clara floating on an adventure through a fantasy world. Yes, it was partly the tutus, but mostly the way the dancers seemed to soar. How graceful yet strong they were. I begged and begged my mother for ballet lessons and as soon as I set foot in that studio, all serious in my pink leotard and tiny ballet shoes, I knew I'd come home. I always felt that way, no matter how hard it got, how tired I was, how painful my feet. Like I was home.'

'So why are you here and not there? Dancers don't have a very long shelf-life, do they? Can you really risk a sabbatical?'

Posy brushed away another tear. 'It stopped being home.' She didn't say any more and, after a quick look at her averted profile, Nico decided not to push any further. He didn't need to. He had his information. Posy Marlowe was at a crossroads—all he needed to do was show her the right way.

They rounded the curve in the coastal path and Villa Rosa came into sight. The famous pink villa was surrounded by a high wall on three sides, the front of the villa overlooking the beach and ocean. The coastal path diverted from the cliff tops to ensure passers-by gave the villa a wide berth, wild meadows running rampant between the walls and the paths, 'Keep Out, private' signs dissuading hikers from taking a short cut through the long grass. Posy had trampled a narrow path from the wall to the path and she set off back along it. 'Sofia would never let us walk through the meadow in May and June,' she said. 'It belongs to the poppies then. We had to take the long way round, through the gates and along the road until it met the path and then turning back on ourselves. Sofia always said it was a sin to step on a wild flower.'

But not a sin to sleep with another woman's husband. Nico stopped the acerbic words before they reached his lips but, he realised, he was going to have to warn Posy not to mention her godmother in front of his grandmother. He might be envisioning a star-crossed lovers narrative for the pair of them but that didn't mean Lady Montague had to befriend Lady Capulet even beyond the grave.

Ivy hung over the faded pink walls, so thickly Nico didn't see the gate until Posy pushed the dark green leaves to one side and revealed the discreet, slim door. Images of his grandfather slipping furtively out rose irresistibly in his mind and Nico was torn between laughter at the ridiculousness of the King sneaking out of the villa like some kind of burglar and icy anger at his grandfather's betrayal, not just of his Queen, but of the whole island. He paused, one hand on the door. Would marrying Posy be worth reviving all that old gossip? Or would their carefully orchestrated happy ever after finally put it to bed? Only time would tell—if she agreed.

The door led into the gardens, now overgrown, faded and crumbling like so much else in the villa. To one side were the garages and in front the famous conservatory with its jewel-coloured glass. The driveway was at the side of the house so that the front had a clear view of the ocean, unhindered by anything as mundane as a path or a driveway or the impressive wrought-iron gates. Gates that had been standing wide open when he had visited the villa earlier today.

'Posy, did you close the gates after me? This morning?'

She started, still lost in a world of her own. 'No, why? I haven't closed them at all. They're so heavy and the lock's stiff. Besides, this is L'Isola dei Fiori. There's practically no crime here.'

'No,' he said grimly. 'But there are photographers. Wait here.'

As boys he and Alessandro had often played at being spies, slipping through the palace as stealthily as possible, searching out the hidden corridors that they knew must be somewhere if they just looked hard enough. Of course they hadn't practised being spies in a creaky house, full of furniture with ludicrously large windows exposing them on every side.

Nico opened the conservatory door and stepped as quietly as possible onto the tiled floor before crossing the vast sunlit room to let himself into the shabby kitchen. He didn't need to go any further. He could hear the noise from here. Banging on the door, voices echoing in through the letter box.

'Miss Marlowe, we just want to talk.'

'Is Prince Nico here?'

'Posy, we are prepared to offer big for an exclusive tell all. My card's on your mat.'

Nico swore under his breath. 'Dammit.' He'd hoped to have had a little more time. It was a good thing he'd made plans for this very situation. Retreating as silently as he had come, he made his way swiftly back to the garden and a wide-eyed Posy. She stood next to the fountain, her dark hair falling out of its loose bun, her legs long and strong in denim cut-offs, the oversized white shirt emphasising her air of fragility. It was just an air, he suspected, remembering the way she'd moved on the beach, the lines of her body twisting and turning, the way she stood poised, balanced, one leg high in the air, the way she cut through the water with clean, strong strokes. But would she be strong enough for what awaited her?

'They're here,' he said brusquely. 'We need to leave. Now.'

CHAPTER SEVEN

POSY SENT A nervous glance Nico's way. He hadn't said a word beyond a curt 'careful' since he'd hustled her away from the villa and down the steep path to the jetty, where he'd helped her into the boat. Posy was torn between admiration that he was one step ahead of the paparazzi by electing to sail to the villa, not drive along the narrow road where they would undoubtedly have found themselves hemmed in by the scarily large pack of photographers and paparazzi—and irritation that he was one step ahead of *her* right up to orchestrating their quick getaway.

She shivered despite the late afternoon sun. Her own sister was an entertainment journalist, used to celebrities and cameras and hustle—and since being linked to Javier had become a paparazzi target in her own right—but this kind of attention was beyond anything Posy had ever experienced.

As for Nico and the crazy plan he had come up with... Suddenly it didn't feel quite so crazy and that scared her more than anything. When a fake love affair and an arranged marriage seemed logical it was a sure sign everything else had turned upside down.

Whoa. Her mind skidded to a stop. Did that mean she was considering agreeing? Of course she wasn't—couldn't—but everything was all happening so fast. Too fast, rapidly skidding so far out of her control she had no idea how she was going to get her life back on track.

She swallowed, willing her voice to come out calm and assertive, not plaintive and wobbling. 'Where are we going?'

Nico barely turned to look at her, all his attention on the wheel as the boat ploughed smoothly through the blue waves. 'The palace.'

'The palace? Is that wise?'

'You'll be safe there.'

L'Isola dei Fiori was a small island and during

her childhood holidays Posy had been to pretty much all of the limited and often old-fashioned sights. She'd sailed out on the old sailing ship, toured the grottos and sea caves, eaten *gelato* at Giovanni's—still renowned as the best ice cream in Europe by those in the know—and spent hours at the old-fashioned fair in the centre of San Rocco, the quaint capital city. Sofia had loved the carousel, riding the faded wooden horses with as much straight-backed grace as if she were on an Arabian steed.

But Posy had never set foot inside the palace even though parts were open to the public, never seen the famous paintings, the celebrated romantic architecture, the graceful spires and spiral stairs more like a fairy-tale castle than a living, breathing building.

Sofia had kept them away from anything and anywhere to do with the Del Castro family. Not for them the feast days and carnivals celebrated with such enthusiasm by the rest of the island or the parades and parties. For the first time Posy realised just how limited her godmother's seemingly glamorous life must have been. Everyone knew who she was and yet she could never be publicly acknowledged.

While Posy herself had suddenly become all too public.

'Maybe I should have stayed put. They'd have gone eventually. If I go to the palace with you then we're making a statement, aren't we? It's as if I'm agreeing to your...' She searched for the right word. She could hardly call it a proposal. 'Your suggestion. But I haven't had a chance to think it through.'

'What do you want, Posy? If this hadn't happened, if we hadn't met, what were you planning to do next?'

She looked down at the water, stirred up into white froth by the boat, and wished for a moment she could dive in and just float there until this was all over. 'I don't know,' she confessed. 'All I ever wanted to do was dance and I haven't decided yet whether I'm ready to stop. I can't make that decision, such a final, life-changing decision, not yet. It's too soon. I might be on a sabbatical but I'm not sure I'm ready to walk away for good.'

'Then give me three months. Three months to convince the world we're falling in love. If after that you decide this isn't for you we'll plan an exit strategy.'

Plan. Exit strategy. Marriage as a boardroom presentation. 'Three months? And then I can walk away?'

'You'll still be linked to me but hopefully we can turn the story around, make you someone people want to be, not someone...'

'Not someone people are giggling about?' It made a crazy kind of sense. 'How would we end it? If I agree? And what about the villa? Will you still pressurise me to sell it to you?'

'We have three months to figure it out. But, Posy, I want you to promise something. If you decide to try, then please really give this engagement a chance. It might not be something you want, something you've ever considered, but it could give you a way forward. You love this island too. Why else would you come here? The island needs some good news, some positive publicity, someone to help me look after it and lead it. You could be that person. Think about it.'

Posy nodded, unable to speak. He was right. The island did have a hold on her heart. It was the place she'd instinctively turned when she had nowhere else to go, nothing to hold onto, no one to turn to. Maybe she could have a purpose here. It was better than no purpose at all.

Three months. It wasn't that long a time. She'd be free before Christmas. Maybe she could give him that. Give herself that. After all, it wasn't as if she had anything more pressing to do. She looked at him, at the set of his jaw, the way his eyes focused on the horizon, the muscles playing in his arms as he kept the boat steady. She'd taken a crazy chance on him once before. Trusted him. Okay, it had all gone horribly wrong but not because of anything he had done—and here he was, trying to make it right.

'Fine, I'll do it. I'll give you three months. But if I do this then you have to be honest with me as well. If it's not working for you then say. After all, you have an entire dossier of other potential wives to choose from.'

He shot her an unreadable look. 'Deal.'

She shifted in her seat. The wind whipped the strands of hair that had fallen from her bun around her face. Posy breathed in, the sea air tasting like freedom. She'd better inhale it while she still could. 'So, what happens next? We announce our engagement straight away?' An unexpected giggle burst from her as she pictured it. Would he stand there and say 'whatever love is' while she stared coyly at her hands?

'Not immediately. First, first we fall in love. Obviously, publicly, and as photogenically as possible. I hope you're ready for your close-up, Miss Marlowe. We're here.'

Any inclination Posy still had to giggle disappeared as Nico expertly steered the boat in between two high, narrow rocks and the boat emerged into a wide bay, the palace perched on top of the cliffs. Guards manned the parapets looking out to sea—not that the island had been invaded during the last two hundred years or so. Before that, however, it had fallen prey to several different empires, which was why, although the official language was Italian, there were Greek, French and the odd bit of British influences across the island.

'Couldn't anyone just sail in?' she asked as Nico headed towards a small harbour on the opposite side of the bay. Several boats were already moored there, including the surviving royal yacht—there had been three but the current King, Nico's uncle, she realised, had sold two—some fancy-looking cabin cruisers and catamarans as well as some more modest boats and dinghies like the one Nico was currently guiding in.

'Technically but the only way up to the palace is heavily guarded and the harbour and beach are monitored and patrolled. We do get the press coming in occasionally but there's very little for them to see here so they can usually be persuaded to leave without too much bloodshed.'

As he spoke Posy saw several smartly dressed soldiers stepping smartly along the harbourside. A welcoming party. 'Oh, no, I'm a mess.' She quickly smoothed back the wisps of hair and pulled her shirt down. 'You should have let me bring some clothes. We had time to pack.' Not that she had anything suitable for a palace. She spent her life in sweat pants and vest tops. Hardly royal attire.

'Don't worry, I called ahead. It's being taken care of.'

'Oh.' One step ahead again.

The boat glided against the dock and Nico threw the rope to one of the soldiers, who caught it in one hand and looped it around a pole. Nico jumped smartly up onto the dock and extended a hand to Posy. She took a deep breath. It was time.

His hand was warm and firm and oddly comforting as he pulled her onto the dock. Posy had an urge to keep hold of it, an anchor in this strange new world. 'Okay?' he asked.

'I think so.'

The soldiers fell in step around them. She could do this. It was just like a ballet, everyone knowing their steps and their place—except Posy, but she was an expert at finding her feet. Nico slanted a glance at her. 'A room's been prepared. I'll take you straight there to wash up and change.'

'And then?'

'And then you meet my family.'

Great. Straight into the lions' den. 'Meeting the parents on the second date.' As she said the words she remembered that his father had died three years ago in a helicopter crash. There had been some whispered scandal; a woman's body had also been uncovered from the wreckage.

Nico seamlessly covered her gaffe. He must have had training: *How to Speak to Tactless Commoners for Beginners.* 'My mother isn't here, you'll be relieved to hear. She lives in France now, splitting her time between Paris and the Riviera. Just my uncle and aunt and my grand-mother.'

'Just the King, Queen and Dowager Queen. Nothing I haven't dealt with one hundred times before. No, wait. That's those girls in your grand-mother's dossier.'

He laughed at that. It was the first time she'd

heard him laugh. It transformed him, lit him up. It would be nice to make him laugh more often…

'Just call them all Your Majesty and defer to my uncle's wisdom and you'll be fine.'

'Is that what you do?'

'I manage the Your Majesty bit, the other I have a hard time with,' he confessed. 'They can be a little intimidating but it's in everyone's interests that this works out so don't let them worry you.'

It was hardly the most reassuring speech Posy had ever heard.

She'd expected hordes of interested onlookers but it was eerily deserted as the guards escorted them past the checkpoint and into the tiled tunnel cut into the cliff, through two sets of security doors, and saluted them as they stepped into a plush lift, just two accompanying them up to the palace. Posy tried not to think about how the lift shaft must be cut into the solid rock as the lift smoothly rose upwards at a stately speed. It was equally deserted when the doors opened into a marble vestibule and they passed through another set of security doors and into the corridor beyond. Either people had been told to keep away or nobody knew she was accompanying Nico back to the palace. She didn't care which one it was, she was just grateful for these last few moments of privacy.

Not counting Nico and the two guards, of course.

She was escorted through a maze of corridors, treading over highly polished marble floors, waxed wooden floors and plush carpets, some passages papered with intricate wallpaper, others painted and edged with intricate plasterwork. No two were the same and as they turned yet another corner Posy knew that she would never ever be able to find her way around here without a ball of thread to mark her way. She walked mutely, following Nico into another lift and along more corridors until he halted outside a white-painted door.

'This wing is the private family wing,' he said. 'We all have rooms here. My uncle and aunt occupy the ground floor, my grandmother's rooms are on the first floor and I am on the floor above you. So you have some privacy. I hope these will suit.' He opened the door as he spoke and stood aside to let Posy precede him in, the guards taking up station on either side of the door as he did so.

Eying the guards nervously—were they really planning on being there all the time and if so what exactly were they there for? To guard her or to keep an eye on her?—Posy stepped inside and stopped still, aware her mouth was hanging open in a most undignified way. 'OMG,' she muttered.

She'd had no idea what to expect—had had no time to consider it—but if she had pictured the private rooms in the old palace she wouldn't have come up with this. She stood in a long, light room, the opposite wall punctuated with four sets of French doors opening out onto a spacious terrace overlooking the sea, the outside space filled with huge flower-filled terracotta pots, a small table and chairs, two loungers and a swinging hammock. The room itself had simple white walls brightened with some huge landscapes and a couple of mirrors and was furnished with a comfortable-looking grey corner sofa and matching love seat, both heaped with red and purple cushions. The seating area was arranged around an open fireplace, a television discreet against the far corner. Tall, filled bookcases took up the far wall, another comfortable-looking love seat sat opposite the windows and a round dining table and four chairs upholstered in a bright flowered pattern were positioned in front of the bookcases. Every available shelf and occasional table held a vase filled with flowers.

The room was bigger than her entire London flat and more luxurious than any hotel room she had ever stayed in. Posy swivelled, eyes wide.

'Like it?'

'It's okay, a little cramped but I'll try to manage.' She did her best to sound nonchalant but knew her wide grin gave her away.

'Your bedroom, dressing room and bath are through there.' He nodded at a white panelled door by the bookcase. 'Your study is through there.' This time he indicated a door by the love seat. 'If you want to change the configuration at all that's fine, just talk to your secretary. You're sharing my grandmother's until we can appoint a permanent one for you.'

'A secretary?'

'To organise your schedule and administrative duties. My grandmother and aunt also have personal ladies-in-waiting but I'd suggest waiting until you know your way around before appointing your own. It can be a political minefield and you don't want to be stuck with a wrong choice—the housekeeper will assign maids to help you until then. The two guards outside your door are part of your bodyguard detail. You'll be accompanied by two at all times.'

Her smile wavered and disappeared. Bodyguards? Ladies-in-waiting? 'I don't really need…'

'Yes. You do. You'll be glad of the help. Dinner is at eight. It's formal dress. Do you want me to ask someone to help you bathe or dress?'

To help her what? 'No. I think I need some time alone.'

His eyes softened. 'I know how it seems. It was always a shock returning home from MIT to all this formality and pomp. You'll get used to it, I promise.'

Posy couldn't imagine ever getting used to guards outside her door but she nodded mutely. Nico strode to the door and paused, gaze intent on hers. 'It's in both our interests to make this work, Posy. If you need anything just let me know.' And then he was gone, leaving Posy alone in a room that she was rapidly realising was more like a luxurious prison cell than a home.

She crossed the room and opened one of the French doors, stepping outside onto the stone terrace, relieved to feel the evening sun on her face, the soft sea breeze on her arms. The terrace stretched out in both directions. It must be accessible from each of her rooms, she realised. She was glad she was on this side of the palace, looking out to sea; it meant she couldn't be overlooked.

A buzz from her pocket startled her. Of course, her phone. She must have a mobile signal here. She pulled it out and sighed. Her phone had picked up the palace wi-fi and it looked as if her inbox was as full as her voicemail. She'd deal with that tomorrow. She couldn't actually face any of it now but she couldn't keep her family waiting any longer. But where to start? What could she say? She took a deep breath and pressed play on her voicemail.

As expected, worried messages from her sisters and her parents, several offers of interviews and representation, which she promptly deleted, and, to her surprise, supportive messages from her flatmates and from a couple of other friends. Posy listened, blinking away tears. She wasn't as alone as she had thought; there were people who cared. She quickly texted Portia, Miranda, Imogen and her parents.

I'm fine. Don't worry. Sorry for everything. Will let you know everything soon. P x

That would hardly put their minds at ease but she simply couldn't talk to them right now. Not until she knew how she felt, could convince them that she was okay. Was less numb. Of course, she hadn't actually seen the pictures yet. She took a deep breath and pulled up her browser and typed in her name.

'Oh, my God.' She sank onto the nearest lounger, putting a hand down for support. 'How could they?'

It was all there. Nico wading naked into the water. Posy dancing, holding a perfect arabesque in the surf. The moment she pulled her dress off. The first kiss. The two of them lying on the sand, naked limbs wrapped around each other. Each picture seared itself onto her retina. How could this be legal? It was so wrong to intrude on something so private and send it out into the world.

There was only one person who could help her right now. Posy closed the browser, wishing she could unsee the images as easily, and pressed Portia's name, relief flooding through her as the call connected.

There was an odd sense of kinship between herself and her oldest sister despite the three-year age gap. Partly it was because Immi and Andie were twins and had always had each other, leaving Posy and Portia together on family days out.

Partly it was because Portia, like Posy, had little interest in aeroplanes, the all-consuming family business and passion. She had built a life away from Marlowe Aviation as a successful journalist in LA—and she'd just married a bona fide A-list film star, which in this day and age almost trumped bagging a prince.

'Posy? Are you okay? Listen to me. Talk to nobody, do you understand? We will be with you tomorrow. Javier's PR person is going to handle everything.'

'Hi, Portia.' To her horror Posy could feel her throat thickening, her chin wobble. *Keep it together, Marlowe,* she told herself sternly. 'I'm so, *so* sorry. Are Mum and Dad furious?'

'You haven't spoken to them?'

'I haven't spoken to anyone. You know what the phone reception is like at the villa.'

'All too well.' Her sister's voice sharpened. 'So where are you? Has anyone seen you?'

'I'm fine, don't worry. I'm...' She paused, aware that once the words were said they couldn't be unsaid, that she would be definitely set on this path. 'I'm with Nico. At the palace.'

'With who? Hang on.' Portia's voice became indistinct as she must have moved the phone away, but Posy could hear the deep rumble of Javier's famously sexy Italian voice replying. 'I'm back. Javier is going to talk to Nico. They're old friends. So what's the plan?'

'Nico wants us to fall in love. I mean, he wants us to look as if we're in love.'

'Interesting. Are you in love with him?'

'No! I mean, I barely know him…'

'Barely seems to be the operative word here. I've seen the pictures.' Portia's voice was dry. 'Why a fake relationship? It all seems a little drastic. My advice is say nothing, keep your head down and return to work. If you're at the palace pretending to be in love then the Internet is going to explode. Are you sure you know what you're doing?'

'He needs to get married, now he's the Crown Prince, and he was planning an arranged marriage anyway so…'

'Rosalind Anne Marlowe. Are you engaged to a prince?' Her sister's voice had risen in pitch to a decibel only bats could comfortably tolerate. 'That's it, I am on my way. You have obviously taken complete leave of your senses.'

'No. Don't come, not yet and, no, I'm not engaged. Yet. I promised to consider giving him three months. To see if we could live together, be married. That's all.'

'That's all? Posy, I don't understand. Four months ago you were almost too busy to come to your own sister's wedding and now you're not dancing, you're living on the island even though I know you should be back in training and you are seriously contemplating marrying a man you don't know. A man you slept with despite not knowing him, which is not like you. What's going on?'

They were all too valid questions. Posy closed her eyes and swallowed. When she said the words out loud then they would be out there. Not just her private shame any more. 'I'm not good enough.' Her voice cracked.

'What do you mean? Of course you are, you're incredible. What makes you say that?'

The tears were freefalling now. 'I wasn't moving on. I should have had solos by now, you know that, but I just wasn't getting picked. I decided to ask for advice and I overheard them say. They said...' She gulped, the sobs tearing out despite her best attempts to swallow them back down.

'Said what, Posy? Darling, try and calm down. You're scaring me.'

Posy took a moment, dashing the tears away with an impatient hand. 'That I had no fire. No life. That I would always have a place in the Corps but I'd never be anything more. I didn't know what to do but I couldn't stay there, Portia. My dream was always to be a soloist, you know that. So I came here to think and when I met Nico I just... I just wanted to prove them wrong. Show myself that I could live. That I had fire.'

'And you got burned. Posy, I have to say when you decide to do something you do it all too thoroughly. Do you really not want me to come right now? I can be with you tomorrow, honey.'

Posy shook her head, forgetting her sister couldn't see her. 'Not yet. Let me figure this out. I appreciate the offer though.'

'If you change your mind...'

'I know. You'll be the first person I call. Thank you, Portia.'

'Do you want me to call Mum and Dad and the twins? They're all pretty worried.'

'Would you? Tell them I'm fine and I'll speak to them as soon as I can. Portia?'

'Yes?'

'I don't want anyone to know. None of it. About why I left London or about the relationship not being real.'

'That's your choice, Posy. But what about Mum and Dad? They'd understand.'

Posy pictured her parents at Andie's wedding, remembering how relaxed her father had looked, ten years younger than when she had last seen him. They'd all been so worried about him after the terrible accident that had killed Rachel, Cleve's pregnant wife, who had been flying one of Marlowe Aviation's new prototypes when she died. The inquest had cleared Marlowe Aviation completely and now Cleve was happily married to Posy's sister, Miranda, their first baby on the way, but the whole incident had left her father badly shaken. How could Posy be responsible for stressing her father when he needed nothing but relaxation and peace?

'I don't want to worry Mum and Dad, and you know how protective Cleve is about Andie now she's pregnant. I can't tell Immi if I'm not telling Andie. They hate keeping secrets from one another. So it's just you. Is that okay?'

'I'm an entertainment journalist, Posy. I know far more secrets than I ever exposed. If you want me to stay quiet then of course I will. They'd all understand but I do see why you want to keep this one quiet for now.'

'Thank you. Love you.'

'Love you too, Rosy-Posy.'

Posy finished the call and collapsed onto the lounger, the sun sore on her swollen eyes. But despite the tears still wet on her cheeks and the ache in her throat she felt better, unburdened.

Maybe she should have spoken to someone earlier about her crisis of confidence. If she had then she might not have ended here, lying on a lounger that looked as if it belonged in a high-end fashion shoot and about to change for dinner with a real life King and his family. But it was a little too late to worry about that.

She swiped her eyes again. She had less than two hours before said dinner and she must look an absolute state; she'd never been able to cry prettily. Time to explore the rest of these lavish apartments and get herself ready for tonight. If there was one thing she understood it was the importance of costume and tonight she was going to need every piece of skill she possessed.

CHAPTER EIGHT

DINNER WAS STILL half an hour away but Nico was ready early. He was pretty sure Posy would need a fortifying drink before the ordeal awaiting them—and he was definitely sure that he did. He pulled at his tie, already hearing his uncle's sarcastic tones. He didn't need reminding that Alessandro would never have messed up in this way. He knew it all too well.

The two guards at Posy's door stood at attention, Nico's own bodyguards waiting at the end of the corridor. If he hadn't dismissed them last night, hadn't snuck out on his own… Was it really only last night? So much had happened in the twenty-four hours since then.

Pushing the dark thoughts from his mind, Nico rapped on the door. None of this was Posy's fault. At first he'd wondered if this was all some kind of elaborate set-up, some kind of trap, the chances of them both skinny dipping on the same deserted shore, the chances of her turning back and propositioning him, the chances of the photographer being there—but her shock had been all too real. She was a victim here, more so than him. And he knew all too well if it weren't Posy here this evening making her formal introduction to his family it would be some other woman a few weeks hence. Better the devil he was getting to know.

'Come in.'

He turned the handle and opened the door, stepping in with a carefully prepared sentence ready, the offer of a drink and a polite compliment, only to stumble to a halt as she turned, illuminated by the last of the summer evening's light pouring in through the windows.

No longer the bare-legged urchin of the day, or the sea-drenched naiad of the night before, Posy personified elegance in a full-length blue cap-sleeved dress, the silky material hugging her shoulders, moulding itself to her small, perfect breasts before gathering just underneath her bust and falling in graceful folds to the floor. She'd left her cloud of silky dark hair loose, simply twisted at the front and fastened back with two silver clips, and her feet were slipped into high-heeled silver sandals. He'd not seen her wear make-up before; it was artfully understated except for the deep red lipstick, accenting every curve of her full mouth.

Posy smiled shyly and gestured at her dress. 'Hi. Will I do? You said formal and this was in the wardrobe but seriously this feels more ball gown than dinner gown to me.'

'You look beautiful,' he said softly.

'Not too much?'

'My aunt wears a tiara to lunch.'

She stared at that. 'Too little? Should I bling it up? Not that I have any bling...'

'No, you look perfect.'

'I had some help, thanks to whichever elves stocked that wardrobe. It's a little creepy to find several outfits, all in my size, waiting for me but as I don't think your uncle and aunt would have appreciated me turning up in yoga pants and a crop top I'm ignoring creepy and going for thankful.' She smiled straight at him then, gesturing to his dinner jacket. 'You scrub up nicely as well.'

'It's a family requirement. We're a little early but I thought you might appreciate a drink before meeting my family.' He held out an arm, feeling more like a character playing a part than he'd ever felt before. 'Shall we?'

Nico devoted the next half-hour to putting Posy at her ease, noting with some relief the colour returning to her cheeks and the sparkle to her eyes. His family wouldn't go easy on her just because she was unprepared and ill at ease; in fact they seemed to scent fear like a pack of wolves and were more than happy to go in for the kill. His father had thrived on the cut-throat atmosphere but his mother had always hated it; no wonder she'd cut and run, moving to France a mere month after being widowed. She'd have been a lot happier if his father had agreed to move there a long time ago, but like a true Del Castro he had refused to leave L'Isola dei Fiori permanently. Just one of the many ways in which they had failed to find a compromise. If his uncle's marriage was a perpetual uneasy truce, his parents' had either been a battlefield or a honeymoon—and Nico had never known which to expect: flying crockery and bitterness or finding them half undressed on the sofa. Either way he had been completely superfluous to their requirements, a spectator to the melodrama of their marriage.

'Your Highness, Miss Marlowe.' A footman was at the door of the small salon to which he had escorted Posy. 'Dinner will be served in five minutes.'

'Thank you,.' He smiled reassuringly at Posy, who had risen to her feet at the words. 'Ready?'

'No, but I don't suppose that makes any difference. Do you do this every evening?'

'Dine in state? No, thank goodness, only when we have guests, which is far too often for my liking, special occasions or when the family needs to meet, but we're just as likely to dine informally in our rooms.'

'Thank goodness. I'm not sure I can eat much

in this dress, it's so tight. I'd fade away if I had to dress up like this every night.'

'My mother said formal meals here were the best dieting technique she'd ever found. If it was a busy week with too many dinners then she would usually order a supper in her rooms afterwards.' As he finished speaking they reached the double doors heralding the entrance to the dining room. Footmen stood at attention on either side and, after a respectful nod, one stepped forward and opened the doors. 'His Royal Highness Prince Nicolas and Miss Rosalind Marlowe.'

Posy's grip tightened on his arm but that was the only outward sign of any concern as she moved in perfect time with him, her face relaxed, smiling politely. She had this, thanks to years of stage training. No matter how nervous she was she knew how to perform. Something his tempestuous mother had never understood.

The tension in his chest lightened. Posy might not have been the obvious choice for his consort but maybe his moment of madness might just work out after all.

The vast dining room was as intimidating as it could be, every chandelier lit and blazing, lighting up the green walls, which were hung with grim still lives mostly featuring dead poultry artfully arranged by a jug or bowls of rotting fruit. Nico and Alessandro had never understood why such off-putting pictures had been hung in a room where people ate—Alessandro had always sworn that when he was king every still life in the palace would be donated to a museum far, far away. The light picked up the gilt edging on the ceiling plasterwork, throwing the various rioting cherubs into hideous relief. Not that things got any better at floor level. The long table was fully made up, crystal candlesticks clashing with the gold cutlery and plates. His family sat like glowering statues at the far end. His uncle upright and unsmiling in the throne-like chair at the head of the table, his aunt at his left and his grandmother to his right.

Nico wasn't sure whether or not to be relieved that they were evidently dining *en famille* this evening. There would be no one outside the family witnessing Posy's first encounter with the Del Castros—but at the same time all gloves would be off. He halted a few steps into the room and bowed stiffly, Posy, less than a second behind him, falling into a graceful curtsey. 'Your Majesty.'

'Sit down, Nico. Next to your aunt. Miss Marlowe, please.' His uncle gestured to his right and a footman pulled out the chair next to his grandmother. Posy hesitated for one moment and then with a nod let go of his arm and walked over to the chair, seating herself smoothly with a polite nod and a quiet but clear and steady, 'Good evening, Your Majesties. It's nice to meet you.' Impressive. His admiration for her courage shot up another notch.

The first few courses went surprisingly well. Posy had excellent table manners and, although she was hardly talkative, she answered any questions put to her with a quiet confidence Nico hadn't expected and the conversation remained on general lines, probing a little into Posy's family and evolving into a discussion about ballet, luckily one of his grandmother's passions. It wasn't until the fruit, cheese and biscuits were served and the footmen waved away that things took a more personal turn.

'So, Nico. I see you behaved in your usual headlong fashion.' His uncle peered at him disapprovingly. 'Am I to understand that you plan to marry this girl?'

'It seems the best option.'

'Hardly the behaviour of the future Queen of L'Isola dei Fiori, is it? Romping naked on the beach with a perfect stranger. I am right in thinking you didn't know each other before yesterday?' His uncle had turned purple. He'd obviously been suppressing his feelings throughout the meal and now, typically, he was erupting with rage.

Posy flushed scarlet and his grandmother set down her cheese knife decisively. Beside him his aunt continued selecting grapes as if nothing was amiss. This was how it always was, the pair of them living parallel lives, never allowing the other to affect them in any way. Nico had never known what was worse—the passion between his parents, which had swung such a fine line between love and hate, or this icy politeness. He'd just known he'd wanted neither. Del Castros weren't known for their happy marriages.

'No. You're not right. Posy and I have known each other for some weeks now.' Nico ignored his grandmother's raised eyebrows and Posy's hastily muffled splutter and smiled pleasantly at his grandfather. 'Her sister married Javier Russo earlier this year. You remember Javier, don't you, Aunt Katerina?'

'Of course. Such a nice boy. He was always such a good friend to Alessandro.' Unlike Nico, she managed to imply without as much as a look in his direction.

His uncle glowered in a way that showed he was still to be convinced. 'What? Where? Thought you were in Boston all spring and summer.'

'I was but I headed to London for a few days.' This was true and luckily Javier and Portia had been there at the same time. His old friend had phoned him a couple of hours ago and, once he'd got his quite considerable feelings about the situation Nico had put his sister-in-law in off his chest, he and Nico had concocted a story that would hopefully stand up to scrutiny. It was quite plausible he and Posy could have met earlier this year. 'We were introduced then and...erm...fell in love. Didn't we, Posy?' He raised his glass to her. She narrowed her eyes at him while picking up her own glass and matching his toast.

'It seemed impossible though. Not only does Nico have his duties here but we were both so busy, Nico in Boston...'

'Finishing my MBA,' he supplied and she thanked him with a swift smile.

'And of course dancing is so all-consuming, we didn't think we would be able to see each other again. But we kept in touch and Nico persuaded me to take a sabbatical and spend a few months on the island as I already own a house here. So we could see if what we had was strong enough. Especially with the, ah, personal connection, we knew any relationship between us would cause some upset.' She shot an apologetic look at Nico's grandmother Nico could swear was genuine. 'Unfortunately we were outed before we could talk to our families. I'm sorry for any embarrassment my actions have brought on the family. This was exactly the kind of situation we were trying to avoid.'

'Our feelings were just too strong,' Nico said helpfully, enjoying how quickly Posy had taken his story and run with it. There was a flicker of that same smile again before she lowered her eyes, the picture of contriteness.

'You'll have to behave with perfect decorum from now on,' his aunt said. 'All eyes will be on you, waiting for you to slip up. Vincenzo and I have worked hard to stop the Del Castro name being a byword for scandal and profligacy. I would hate for all our work to have been in vain. This is exactly the kind of situation which could have been avoided. It's your grandfather all over again. Or your father. If he'd shown some sense and decorum then he'd be here right now, but even in his death he brought shame on the family and on your poor mother.'

Nico sensed his grandmother tense and his grip

tightened on his wine glass. His uncle got angry and said exactly what was on his mind no matter how offensive, but Nico would rather that than listen to his aunt's colourless voice dripping poison. How she had managed to birth and raise a sweet-tempered, warm-hearted boy like Alessandro he had no idea. All he knew was that since her beloved son's death she was worse than ever, especially where he was concerned.

He swallowed. 'We have no intention of behaving in any other way,' he said tightly.

'The PR department are all over it,' his uncle cut in. 'The two of you have a full diary of engagements designed to show you in love and committed, some personal, some formal, including the September ball in five weeks' time. We will announce your engagement that evening.'

Posy's surprised gaze flew to meet his at the pronouncement. Nico tried to smile reassuringly at her but it was hard to muster the enthusiasm. He could feel the bars closing in, smothering him. Duty, country, family. Everything he was, everything he wanted irrelevant—and he'd be dragging the elfin girl opposite down with him.

'So we're in love, are we?' Posy kicked off the too tight heels with an inward sigh of relief and turned to glare at Nico, who was leaning against her wall, arms folded and navy eyes gleaming with sardonic humour.

'Madly.'

'It was a good save,' she admitted. 'It would have been nice to have had a heads-up though.'

'You didn't need it. That was a very impressive show you put on there.'

'Good to know all those character, improvisation and mime classes came in handy. When did you speak to Javier?'

'Just before I escorted you to dinner. He and Portia had planned it all. They were just checking dates to make sure we wouldn't get caught out. He texted me while we were at dinner to let me know it was a go. I would have warned you it was a possibility only I didn't want to raise your hopes. I didn't expect my uncle to be quite so direct. No, that's not quite true, I did expect it. I just hoped he might show some better manners.'

'No, he was justified in what he said.' Posy realised how very tired she was, the adrenaline that had kept her alert draining away and with it all her energy. She collapsed onto the sofa, the folds of her dress frothing up around her. 'I did behave badly. I don't know what came over me. I've never done anything like that before.'

'You didn't act alone. And, Posy. Don't let anyone make you feel that last night was wrong or sordid. The person who sold those photos is the one who should be ashamed.'

'Right up until I saw those photos it was the most beautiful moment of my life. The one and only time I acted on instinct, without thinking.' Had she just said that out loud? She cringed, more exposed than when she had seen him in the water and realised she wasn't alone in the evening sea.

Nico didn't respond immediately, his face carefully blank, and Posy searched for something to say to lighten her statement. Beautiful moment? What had she been thinking? He pushed off the wall and walked purposefully over to her, taking her hands in his.

'We're in this together. It's not what either of us wanted but I won't let you face it alone. And not just because your brother-in-law thinks he's a Hollywood hard man.'

Posy inhaled, the pressure of his fingers entwined in hers a strange comfort. She looked at him, at the sharp lines of his face, the long-lashed eyes, and her stomach folded. He was the most glorious man she had ever seen, strong and solid with a mouth made for sin. And he was both hers and not hers. Possibly, if she agreed, her partner in a *pas de deux* for life and yet it would always be for show, every step a fake. 'How can you face it? An arranged marriage? Don't you want to fall in love?'

'Do you?' he countered.

'I don't know,' she said honestly. 'I hadn't really thought about it before my sisters married. My life was so full, so busy. Love was a distraction.' But it was a whole other thing to take it completely off the table, to promise to be faithful to a man who didn't want her love, who didn't love her.

'It's all a gamble, Posy. My parents married for love, my aunt and uncle because she had the right name and the right fortune but they had no shared interests, nothing beyond a tepid liking. Neither couple managed anything close to happiness. It's not easy, life here. Common goals, a common duty, these are the ways to survive a life in the spotlight. It's hard enough without adding emotion into it. But I think we might have respect. Liking. Attraction.' His eyes darkened on the last word and her chest tightened. 'We have that, don't we?'

It was too late for coyness, for denial. She felt him with every part of her whenever he was near her; she tingled with awareness of him. Her mouth remembered the taste of him, salt sweet on the tip of her tongue, her hands knew the feel of him, the play of muscles under her hand, the strength of him. Her breasts ached with the memory of his touch, his kiss. Her throat was thick with need, with wanting. He was the one constant, the one bridge between the Posy she was and the Posy she was going to have to be and she wanted to hold on, to lose herself in him.

'Yes,' she whispered. 'I think we do.'

'We have to play at being in love.' His thumb was moving, caressing the sensitive spot at her wrist, and a jolt shot through her at the contact. 'We might as well enjoy it. Put on a good show.'

'I think we already did that.' It was hard to formulate the words while his thumb made those lazy circles, while his eyes smiled at her with such intent.

'You'll have to hold my hand, kiss me, laugh at my jokes. Gaze at me adoringly.'

'Luckily I'm a good actress so I might manage that.' She gasped as his hand slipped lower, his thumb caressing her entire forearm now. How could one touch on one small area of skin set her whole body alight like this? Sparks were fizzing around her veins, fireworks going off with each swirl.

'We might want to practise.'

'The laughing?' Posy had no idea how she was

managing to speak when all her mouth wanted to do was find his.

'The kissing.'

She couldn't answer; all words were gone. She was incapable of thought, of anything but feeling as his hands slipped up her arms to her shoulders, one feather-light touch stroking her throat, and she arched like a satisfied cat before finally his mouth was on hers, as warm and demanding and sweet as she remembered, his body pressing on hers with a glorious heaviness. Posy's hands buried themselves in the nape of his neck, pulling him even closer until she wasn't sure where she began, where he ended, pulling impatiently at layers of clothes, wriggling out of that darn, tight-as-a-glove dress until finally there was nothing separating them. Finally she could surrender to his hands, his mouth, the demand of her body as she soared higher than she ever had before, all memories obliterated by the here and now.

CHAPTER NINE

IT WAS ONLY early September and already change was in the air. The sun was setting a little later, the evenings were that little cooler, the wind whipping their faces and ruffling Posy's hair had an unexpected bite unthinkable even a few days earlier.

Nico steered his sports car around one of the island's famous hairpin bends, the mountains rearing up on one side, the sea a dizzying drop below on the other. Posy leaned back in her seat, a relaxed smile on her face, her eyes hidden by huge sunglasses—and if her knuckles were a little white then that was only to be expected. The mountain drive could test the hardiest of nerves.

It was a good thing he was keeping his eyes on the road and not on the enticing dip in her sundress. His own test of nerves.

They were supposed to be in love and, Nico supposed, lust came close. He hadn't expected this to happen, even after the circumstances of their first encounter. He'd told himself that Posy needed time to adjust to their situation, that it would be wrong to let her think he could or would give her more than affection and respect. He'd reminded himself how much less experienced she was than him and that he absolutely mustn't take advantage of that—but she'd looked so lost, so alone, so vulnerable when she'd told him that their night together had been beautiful, that he'd ached to comfort her the only way he knew how. He might still have held back, done the right thing, if she hadn't looked at him with need in those big eyes, if her skin hadn't been so soft under his touch.

He didn't know if the physical intimacy made things easier or harder. He did know that now they'd started it seemed silly to stop. Everyone in the palace expected him to spend the night in her rooms. It would cause unwanted gossip and speculation if he stayed away.

So he didn't. And although he still didn't know her favourite food or book or movie he did know the way she liked to be kissed, to be touched. He knew that she slept splayed out like a child, somehow managing to take up far more than her fair share of both bed and covers; he knew the way she eased into the day, a minute at a time. He knew how she looked in the middle of the night, eyes closed, lips parted, totally relaxed.

It was unnerving, knowing so much about a person. Even more unnerving to realise she must know the same things about him. That there must be times when she watched him sleep, saw him vulnerable and unaware.

Everything he was trying to avoid.

The days were a little easier. He had his work: meeting with consultants, tour companies and investors, as well as the more ceremonial side of his role and the other demands the palace loaded onto his increasingly heavy schedule. Posy was still a guest in the palace but, once the September Ball was held and their engagement announced, she would have a few carefully selected and managed public appearances. For now her stay in the palace was being treated as a 'family affair'. Not that she was on any kind of holiday. The time she didn't spend with him on an orchestrated 'date' she spent being educated in everything from the correct way to address a diplomat's mother to Italian lessons to an intensive course in L'Isola dei Fiori history, geography and customs.

She bore the intense workload without grumbling—as she explained to him she was used to early mornings and to being in class at least eight hours a day. As long as she wasn't expected to stay still for too long she could cope with hours of instruction and when it got too much she, like him, escaped to the gym. More than once he found her there, engrossed in her stretches and exercises, completely unaware of his presence as she moved her body through routines she obviously knew as instinctively as language. The first time Nico came across her he watched for a while as she stood, straight-backed, feet apart, one hand steadying itself on the rail, the other curved in front, balanced on one impossibly slim, impossibly strong leg, the other raised at an impossible angle.

It felt even more intimate than watching her sleep. He'd moved soundlessly away to pound out his energy on the running machine and made sure to avoid the gym when she was there.

'So what's the plan?' Posy's soft voice interrupted his reverie and Nico roused himself, glad to shelve his thoughts for the time being.

'Plan? We're having a spontaneous day out on one of the island's most famous beauty spots where we may just get photographed having fun, and the photos sold to both demonstrate how respectably in love we are and, conveniently, what a romantic destination the island is.'

'Two-in-one day trip.'

'The best kind.'

Over the last couple of weeks he and Posy had visited several picturesque spots, the palace PR ensuring that friendly photographers were tipped off as to their whereabouts. He'd taken Posy out to visit some of the enchanting rocky islands that lay less than a mile off L'Isola dei Fiori's coast, the two of them all too visible on the small sailing boat as they sunbathed, picnicked and kissed. They'd spent a day in San Rocco's enchanting medieval old town, where they'd wandered hand in hand through the colourful market. Nico had bought a peach from a delighted stallholder to present to his lady before enjoying the rides at the small carnival, which might keep knuckles unwhitened but held such olde worlde charm. A photo of them embracing by the famous waterfall, said to have been formed from Venus's tears, went viral almost instantly. The PR team were constantly monitoring all references to the pair and in just over a fortnight the mood had turned from prurient to curiosity and romance. The public were buying it.

Not only that, but enquiries for accommodation on the island for the next season were already up significantly on this year. The plan was working.

And in less than a month their engagement would be announced.

Posy's whole family had been invited to the September Ball; not only were her parents taking time out of their busy schedule to attend, but all three of her sisters complete with their husbands and fiancés would also be there. 'We'll have to fake it like never before,' she told him when the news was relayed to them. 'Portia's the only one who knows the truth and I want to keep it that way. One hint that we're not in this for real and they'll whisk me away before you can say royal wedding.'

'You're an adult,' he'd protested. 'They can't make you do anything you don't want to do.'

'I just don't want them to be disappointed in me.' But it wasn't her words that rocked him back on his heels. It was the wistful look in her eyes. She'd agreed to give him three months and he sensed she would keep her word but she was still unconvinced about the marriage, even if she was enjoying some of the benefits of royal life, including a knockout wardrobe. Every time she was photographed looking immaculate it triggered another delivery of clothes. On his aunt's advice she accepted a few; the rest were sold off to benefit the Del Castros' chosen charities. But not even the most exquisite dress had made her happier than a box that had arrived from London this morning, a box filled with pale satin shoes with blocked edges. 'My own shoes,' she'd gasped, her eyes suspiciously wet. 'Look, Nico. Pointe shoes.'

He had managed not to point out that she would have little use for them now. 'Surely you have hundreds of pairs,' he'd said instead as she'd picked one of the slender slippers out of the box and cradled it.

'These were made just for me. This is the make I prefer and they're the perfect fit. We always get several pairs at a time so we can break them in, sew ribbons on, darn them.' She'd turned the pale satin shoes over in her hands, her fingers caressing them.

'You have to darn them?' He wasn't entirely sure what darning even was. 'Don't you have people to do that for you?'

She'd swatted him away, appalled. 'Every dancer sews and darns her own shoes, no matter who she is.'

Unnecessary work, antiquated customs, a rigid hierarchy? No wonder she fitted in so well at the palace. Even his grandmother had conceded that Posy had pretty manners, although she was still wary of Posy's close connection to her great rival.

Posy shifted in her seat, a sure sign she was about to say something she was unsure would be well received. 'Nico, I'm arranging for my parents to stay at the Villa Rosa, my sisters too.'

He kept his eyes on the perilous road. 'We have plenty of space at the palace.'

'An entire wing's worth of space, I know. But the Villa Rosa is really special to all my family, all of my sisters stayed there this year, we all love it and, no matter what happens with us, you and me, the villa won't be part of that. If we...' She paused. She did that a lot, he'd noticed, happy enough with the present-day deception but unable to talk about their possible future together. 'If things go the way you're planning,' she said instead, 'then I won't need the villa. And if we don't.... If after the three months we decide it's not working then it would be a little awkward for me to come here to the island for a while, let alone live here. So you can have the villa for your hotel. It needs more spending on it than I could manage and it's too beautiful for just one person to own. If it's a hotel then many people will get the opportunity to fall in love with it. But I want one last time there with my family around me.'

'You're planning to stay there too? Is that wise?' The island still teemed with journalists and photographers, all eagerly covering this most scandalous of royal relationships, and although that was exactly what Nico had hoped would happen it did mean Posy had no privacy and was followed everywhere she went.

'I think I'll be okay. It was built to keep out prying eyes, after all, and with my family, my sisters' partners, Javier's bodyguards and my own bodyguards I think I might be able to sleep soundly at night. The only thing is...'

'What is it?'

'If we were to go ahead and marry then the villa can be my engagement gift to you,' she said in a rush. 'I have nothing else suitable. I mean, what do you buy a man who has everything he needs?' The words shot through him piercing and cold. Everything he needed? Materially yes. Physically Nico knew he was blessed with good genes, a strong body, better than average brains. But everything? He'd put his research aside the day Alessandro died. And, he realised, there was no one who cared if he lived or died save what it meant to the island's succession. After all, his own mother hadn't seen him in two years.

'But if we don't you want compensating? That seems fair.'

'Thank you. I wouldn't ask but the villa is all I have.'

'You could sell your story. You'd make your fortune.'

She turned to face him then, eyes wide with indignation. 'I could *what*? I can't believe you would even *think* that I would do that to you.'

'You wouldn't be the first.' Nico could hear the bitterness coating his voice and forced himself to lighten up. 'Or even the second.'

He started as she laid a cool hand on his arm. 'Who?'

'It's probably easier to tell you who didn't,' he said, keeping his voice light. 'There's quite a list, starting with the first girl I slept with, my first girlfriend at MIT, several of the girls I dated since. More than several.' The latter didn't matter. Once Nico had worked out that it was his name, his title that attracted the girls the later betrayal was inevitable. It was the first two that really had got him. He'd thought that they were real, that they saw beyond the image, beyond the Prince.

'Oh, don't look so horrified,' he said, glancing over with a grin. 'It goes with the territory. A family with my reputation is always in the headlines. Might as well make sure it's for the fun we had rather than the fun we didn't have. Why do you think we investigated you so thoroughly? Made sure there was nothing in your past to hurt you? The last thing you needed was the *I deflowered Princess Posy up against the ballet barre* headlines. Luckily your relationships were not only brief but you chose well. None of the gentlemen concerned are at all interested in speaking to the press.'

'It wasn't against the barre, thank you very much,' Posy protested and, as he'd intended, she stopped looking at him with soulful, sad eyes.

His relief was short-lived.

'Who was she?'

'Which one?'

'The first?'

'It was a long time ago,' he said, hoping she'd take the hint, but although he steadfastly refused to look at her and she didn't speak he could feel her gaze, compassionate and curious. He sighed. 'She was French, a friend of my cousin's on my mother's side. She was a couple of years older than me, a model, had acted in a couple of films in a semi-unclad love-interest way. I was sixteen. Obviously I was besotted. She went back to France, released a single and made sure she got all the publicity she needed.'

'What did your family say?'

'My grandfather called me a true Del Castro, my father mentioned he'd have liked to have known her better himself, my uncle told me I was a disgrace and a reprobate. All the women pretended it had never happened. A standard Del Castro scandal.'

'What did Alessandro say?'

Nico's chest tightened as the heaviness of grief descended once more. Even after two years it was never far away. 'That he was sorry this had happened to me.'

'Me too, although she sounds like a right cow and you were definitely better off without her.'

He couldn't help smiling at the indignation in Posy's voice. 'I know that now, I knew that when I was seventeen, but at sixteen? Then I thought my heart was broken.'

Not broken, just cracked a little. Then cracked again and once again until he'd simply hardened it so no betrayal could ever hurt him again.

'What about Alessandro?'

'What about him?' he asked warily.

'He was a Del Castro too. Did no one he ever dated or slept with sell their story? I mean, he was what? Thirty-one, thirty-two when he died and single? There must have been something scandalous.'

'No, not really.' He paused, inhaled and then said the words he had never said to another living soul. 'Alessandro fell in love when he was seventeen and as far as I know was completely faithful until the day he died.'

'He...he was? But why on earth wasn't he married? I mean, if a complete commoner like me is an acceptable wife then surely...' She stopped and when he risked a quick look she was staring at him, comprehension on her face. 'It wasn't a she, was it?'

'Guido,' he confirmed. 'He's a Captain in the Guard. I'll introduce you. You'll like him.'

'Who knew?'

'Me. No one else as far as I know. Guido knew that if it got out he'd lose his job, Alessandro that the scandal might be too much even for L'Isola dei Fiori.'

'Scandal? I can see it might have caused a stir...'

'This isn't London, Posy. This is a small, religious, deeply conservative island. It's improving, becoming more tolerant but we don't yet have equal marriage—that's something I hope to change one day. So the chances of them accepting a gay king? Right now that's inconceivable.'

'What was he planning to do?'

'He was hoping to abdicate.'

'What was stopping him? I can see your uncle would have been upset but surely that was better than living a lie?'

'Me,' he said bleakly. 'I was stopping him. He knew how much I hated the duties and responsibilities that come with being a Del Castro, knew that the last thing I wanted was to be King. He kept steeling himself to break up with Guido, to marry and get an heir to let me off the succession hook but he always found a reason to put it off for another year. I knew how miserable he was at the thought of marriage but I never told him it was okay, never accepted my role as his heir.' His smile was tight. 'Ironic, isn't it? Here I am anyway and yet he never had that peace of mind. I never *gave* him that peace of mind. Now Guido mourns, unacknowledged and alone, and I'm Crown Prince anyway. Alessandro's sacrifice was for nothing.'

CHAPTER TEN

POSY SEARCHED FOR words of comfort and came up blank. This was beyond her world, beyond her knowledge. She'd been a guest at several gay weddings, attended christenings for the offspring of same-sex parents; it was easy to forget that not every couple, every person had that acceptance, that in some families, in some places, who you loved could still be considered a sin, was still thought wrong.

'I'd love to meet Guido.' It was all she could think of to say and it was nowhere near enough. Poor Alessandro, caught between duty and the man he loved—and poor Nico, knowing that a word from him might free his cousin and yet unable to utter it, to take on that burden willingly.

'I'll organise dinner in a few nights' time.'

'Good.' She stared out at the scenery, heart ach-

ing. In a few minutes they would pull up somewhere beautiful and hold hands, laugh, gaze
soulfully at each other, kiss...usually she quite
enjoyed it. Nico was fun to be with, attentive—
and lovely to kiss. It wasn't exactly a chore, more
a perfectly choreographed performance. But right
now the thought of the pretence sickened her.
'Can we do something else?' She turned to him,
not even knowing what she was going to say
until the words came out. 'Something you love?
Something for us, not for the cameras?'

Something for us. She cringed inside as the
words echoed through her brain in all their need-
iness but Nico didn't comment, just gave her a
quick hard look then nodded.

Posy sat back and stared out at the scenery but,
even though the sun reflected off the impossibly
blue sea and a company of gannets rose high in
the distance before plummeting deep into the wa-
tery depths, she barely noticed the wild beauty.

Nico had just shared something of himself with
her.

Her stomach twisted and she turned to stare

fixedly out of the window, hoping her face didn't betray her thoughts. She'd known him for just over a fortnight, plunged straight into this un-natural intimacy, all their spare time spent to-gether, their nights.

Heat pooled deep down and her hands tight-ened their grip on her bag. Oh, dear God, the nights. Nothing in her admittedly limited expe-rience had prepared her for those...

She'd only had a few brief relationships, un-willing to spend frivolously time that could be used to improve her dancing, and had met them all through work. She'd liked them well enough but once the first 'butterflies and speeded heart rate' stage had passed she'd had little incentive to keep the relationships going; and nice as the physical side had been it hadn't compared with the adrenaline rush of being on stage. *Nice*. Such a telling word. And nothing about this situation was nice.

It wasn't that Nico was ever anything but po-lite and attentive, because he was both of those things. It wasn't that she didn't feel attracted to him because—oh, my goodness—she really was. But polite and attraction weren't enough to stake her life on. Her future.

She'd agreed to the three months. Agreed to keep an open mind as to their future and she'd meant it. She had no other pressing options so why not see how a permanent role on L'Isola dei Fiori worked out? But open-minded or not she hadn't really—didn't really—expect that at the end of the three months she was going to say yes. Because that would be insane.

And that was an easy decision to make and keep to while Nico stayed being perfectly polite—even if just the thought of the sex made her toes curl and her throat close up. But when he opened up, revealed something personal, confided in her? Well, that shed a new light on everything, on him, on the darkness inside him, a light Posy desperately didn't want or need. Because she could survive this, she could walk away head high, as long as her heart was intact. But she was a mere novice at this game and too many conversations like the one they'd just had, too much intimacy? That would make things very difficult for her indeed.

'We're nearly there.'

'Great.' She grimaced as her voice came out more like a squeak than the casual, relaxed tone she'd been aiming for. She straightened and looked around. Nico had taken her inland, back into the national park although it wasn't a part she recognised, wooded and far nearer the mountains than the Villa Rosa. He pulled off the road and drove down the kind of unmade track that would be uncomfortable in a four-by-four but was teeth-rattling in a low sports car. Posy hung onto the door and gritted her teeth, blowing out a heartfelt sigh of relief when he finally pulled to a stop under some trees. They were in a car park of sorts, grassy and unmarked, but several other cars were parked there in an orderly fashion and a definite path led off from one side.

Posy opened her door cautiously, searching for a clue as to where they were or what they were there to do. Nico's whole demeanour seemed lighter, freer, as he swung himself out of the car, eyes lit up with excitement, more like the teasing, carefree man she'd met in the sea rather than the dutiful, honourable Prince. Her heart stuttered. 'Careful, Posy,' she muttered. That teasing, carefree man had led her into trouble once before...

The four-by-four that held her two bodyguards and Nico's own detail pulled into the car park behind them. It was funny how quickly she forgot to notice them, not even aware of their constant presence on their tail. Nico held up a hand to tell them to stay where they were and to her surprise they obeyed with no more remonstration than a sharp look. Obviously this was somewhere Nico came often. Somewhere considered safe.

'This way.' He paused only to lock the car before setting off at a pace down the grassy track. Posy had dressed with care for the day's visible date wandering through one of L'Isola dei Fiori's picturesque villages, purchasing some souvenirs from the wood carver and lunch in the village square, and so was wearing an orange silk skirt that flared out to her knees and a white, sleeveless, broderie anglaise blouse, block-heeled sandals on her feet. Hardly an outfit for a woodland walk. She paused for a moment and then followed him. A ruined pair of shoes was a small price to pay for a day away from the cameras.

She was horribly aware that if she wanted to avoid another opportunity to get to know the real Nico then the last thing she should be doing was playing hooky with him, asking him to choose something for them to do. But as she fell into step beside him, as her arm brushed his, as he gave her a quick grin she couldn't find it in herself to be sorry or to suggest they went back to the original plan. One day and then they would be back on schedule, back to playing their parts. What harm could one day do?

The track was in better shape than she'd expected, the grass mown down and the ground smooth underfoot. The trees on either side cast a much-appreciated shadow over her as she walked, relieving some of the oppressiveness of the hot late summer's day. The path curved away in front of them and as they followed it a clear blue lake came into view, a few small wooded islands breaking up the smooth water. It didn't seem to be a huge lake, less than half a mile across and another half a mile to one side; the other end was still out of view. It was very attractive, the edges ringed with golden beaches, the trees a green backdrop behind. 'Oh, how pretty. Almost too pretty to keep to ourselves. This is exactly the kind of place you want potential tourists to see.'

'We can come again with cameras,' Nico assured her. He shot her an amused glance. 'And appropriately dressed as well.'

Posy shook her skirt out with a flounce. She might not be in full on trek-proof walking gear but she was more than adequately dressed for a wander around a lake...

Or not. She came to a standstill as the rest of the lake and lakeside opened up before her, wider and longer than she had imagined—and instead of the quiet walkers' paradise she had been expecting the lake was filled with sails and crafts, from small sailboats only big enough for one to kayaks, paddleboards to windsurfs. Two long jetties jutted out, boats bobbing alongside attached by short ropes, and kayaks were pulled up high on the beach. A low, long building was positioned behind the jetties and behind that a larger car park, this one full of cars. Picnic tables were dotted all around the building and the smell of fried food wafted enticingly from a serving window, a queue snaking back several feet.

Nico turned with a grin of anticipation. He looked as if he'd come home. 'Like it?'

Posy stared. 'I guess. I mean, everyone looks like they're having fun.' She hadn't expected people, especially not so many of them.

'So, what do you fancy? Pick your ride.'

'Erm…what do you usually do?' she hedged.

'If I'm feeling lazy I might take out a paddle board, if I don't want to think I usually pick a sail boat because that keeps me pretty occupied and if there's some issues I need to work out I'll kayak. I belonged to a watersports club in Boston,' he clarified. 'I like climbing as well but this was right on the river, easy to do after I'd finished in the library so a great way to work out. In winter I skied, obviously.'

Obviously. How, in two weeks living at close quarters with him, had she not realised he was an adrenaline junkie? *Come on, Posy,* she scolded herself. He was skinny dipping the first time you saw him and even if you didn't expect to get caught he must have known full well there was a chance he'd be followed. Of course he's an adrenaline fiend.

'I don't ski. Or climb. Or do any of these things. I've always had to be careful of torn muscles or broken limbs.'

'But you must kayak. All those summers at Villa Rosa. That beach is perfect for water sports.'

She shook her head. 'Petrol head sisters, remember? If there was anything that needed steering, revving or manoeuvring then they were there first. At first I was too little to care and then I was too worried about muscles in the wrong places so I didn't mind sitting back while they rowed or steered. And since I joined the company it's not been an issue. I've not been near a lake or beach except to sunbathe or walk or have a sedate swim.'

'So what do you do to relax?'

She took a deep breath, the lead weight back in her stomach. 'I dance.'

The words hung there for a moment and then she added, 'But I'll need something else now, I guess, and I don't need to worry about developing the wrong muscles so what do you suggest?'

'A kayak,' he said promptly. 'Let's test your balance. And we can get a double so you don't go drifting off across the lake and need rescuing.'

'I admire your faith in me. The only thing is, I know these clothes were free but I still don't want to waste the designer's generosity by taking a silk skirt into the water.' Not to mention the certainty that her blouse would get see-through the second it was wet. Just because they hadn't arranged for a camera to be here didn't mean there wouldn't be any candid shots leaked and Posy was quite sure the world had seen quite enough of her nipples, thank you very much.

Nico nodded towards the shack. 'They have a

shop. Go get yourself kitted out. I have an account.'

Twenty minutes later Posy had been kitted out in a bikini, which she wasn't entirely sure covered much more than the nothing she'd worn just over two weeks ago, a pair of tiny board shorts and a cropped T-shirt. If she'd been able to fit in them she would have preferred to choose from the men's baggier and lengthier range but the one T-shirt she'd tried had dwarfed her and the smallest shorts had slid right off. The appreciation in Nico's eyes went some way towards mitigating her feeling of exposure but not much.

'If I become Queen I am going to decree that everywhere should sell clothes that cover women properly,' she said, pulling the T-shirt down and realising she was either exposing her bare stomach or her cleavage but there was no way of hiding both.

Nico's eyes slid over her approvingly. 'I'll immediately rescind it,' he said. 'In fact all women should dress like this all the time.'

'Hardly practical. I've been here on the island

in February before and it may not be London cold but it's chilly. Ugh, this is ridiculous, I feel like I'm dressed for a swimsuit-calendar photoshoot.' She tried tugging the shorts up and, when they still didn't budge over her hip bones, started stomping towards the beach, resisting the temptation to wrap her arms around her torso.

Nico watched her, obviously bemused. 'Posy, you're a dancer. I've seen pictures of you in outfits far scantier than that, flesh-coloured leotards, carnival costumes all glitter and sequins and nothing else. I agree it's wrong not to give women the choice to cover up and not everyone is comfortable in such clothes, but why are *you* so het up?'

It was a good question and Posy paused on her way down to the water, her newly acquired flip-flops uncomfortable on her feet. 'Maybe because all those leotards are just costumes. No one looks at me in those and sees my body as anything but an instrument. I was always proud of my body.' She looked down, at her taut stomach, muscles clearly defined, at her strong legs. 'I worked hard at it, to shape it, to make it move the way I needed it to. But that night, when they took those photos, it stopped being something I was proud of.' It had become something shameful instead. She gulped, barely able to say the words.

'I just don't want to be photographed like that again. Exposed like that again.'

She bit her lip and looked down again. She'd been angry, at first, and from there whirled into this ridiculous over-the-top life of fake courtships and language lessons and never having time to think or be alone. There hadn't been time to really process what had happened, time to admit how violated she felt even to herself. But as she stood here, in the ridiculously tiny shorts with an even tinier bikini underneath, the fear of being photographed like this, leered over, laughed at, judged, chilled her.

Nico stood stock-still then turned and went back into the shack. He was only gone a short while, a minute at most, before he emerged wearing one of the bright surf T-shirts, holding his short-sleeved shirt in his hand. 'Here,' he said, handing it to Posy. 'Wear this.'

The shirt was a little crumpled, warm from the sun and his body heat, and as she drew it on she could smell his scent, the slightly salty, musky essence of him. It was large on her, baggy as she knotted it across her stomach. It was comforting. 'Thank you,' she said huskily.

It was a sweet, thoughtful gesture. Posy shivered. This day was proving to be full of surprises and every one pulled her in deeper than she'd had any intention of going.

'Here.' Nico broke into her thoughts as he tossed a life jacket over to her. 'This will cover you up even more nicely.'

She took the luminous orange bulky inflatable and shrugged into it, glad to have something to occupy her hands, a reason to bow her head so he couldn't see her face. 'Okay, Captain,' she said. 'I'm ready.'

If Posy hadn't been sitting in front of him, paddle clumsy in her uncertain hands, digging away at the water with more enthusiasm than skill, then Nico would have set out at top speed, pushing every muscle to the max as he forged through the water, burning every regret, every second thought away with sweat and searing muscles. Instead the pace was as sedate as a maiden aunt on an afternoon stroll, his attention focused on keeping the boat upright as Posy pushed it this way and that, squealing as she did so. 'Sorry!' 'Oops!' 'My bad!'

'I thought a ballerina would have perfect balance,' he said. Unable to resist teasing her.

'I have. It's this boat that's off...'

'Yeah, yeah. Blame the boat.'

He tried to concentrate on the stroke, on matching her efforts, but instead her earlier admission rang in his head, the picture of her downcast eyes as she'd practically whispered her words, the knowledge she no longer celebrated her beautiful, perfectly honed body but sought to hide it instead. The way she'd tugged at that ridiculous T-shirt as if somehow with sheer force of will she could make it bigger.

Before him she had loved her body, what it could do, how it made her feel. Now she was ashamed. And he'd had no idea.

The last couple of weeks had been such a whirlwind and she had slotted into the role assigned to her with such grace and ease it was easy to forget it wasn't a role she had applied for at all. She hadn't complained once, had shed no tears as far as he could see, had borne with good grace any off-colour remarks or questions thrown at her by the pursuing reporters. He'd had no idea she was struggling, that that night had left scars that were still all too raw.

He should have known. He knew what it was like to be vulnerable, exposed. And yet watching her pose for the cameras, the way she prettily flirted with him in public, the way she gave him space in private, the way she welcomed him into her bed—or on the sofa or floor—he'd had no idea she was hurting at all. He'd promised himself that no matter what he would be a good partner. Less than a month in and he was failing already.

But how could he have known? What was normal to him was impossible to anyone else and it was so easy to forget that he was the one whose life was off kilter. He lived in a family where divorce was impossible, admitting to your sexuality even more so. He lived in a family who thrived on affairs, on scandal, whose every move was examined in tabloids across the world. Those photographs for him had been annoying, sure, but more because of the timing, less the subject matter. He had already been exposed in public in every way possible. 'Sweet, enthusiastic but clumsy' his first girlfriend had dismissed his early love-making efforts as, for all the world to read. Five years later some nearly forgotten woman had upgraded him to 'blissful'. He'd barely noticed.

But Posy hadn't grown up in this world, in his world, and just because she hadn't made a fuss about the photos evidently didn't mean they hadn't hit her hard. She might have made the first move that night on the beach but she had had no idea who he was, no idea of the risk she was taking, the risk he was letting her take. If she married him she'd harden; she would have to. The process had already begun. And he hated himself for the role he had played, was playing, in the painful process.

He pushed the thoughts away, upping the pace to Posy's evident surprise, guiding the kayak through the clear water towards the furthest island. 'That's it,' he told her. 'Keep it at that angle, let the paddle slide in, deeper than that. Well done, Posy, that's great.'

'It's harder than it looks,' she panted. 'Although we do seem to be going a little faster than everyone else.' She gave a longing look at the kayak they passed, the girl reclining in the front smiling up at the boy lazily paddling them sedately over the lake. 'Look, they're taking time to enjoy the view.'

'I thought you were fit.'

'I *am* fit, different muscles, that's all. Remind me to challenge you to a workout contest some time.' Nico wasn't sure he wanted to take her up on the offer, now when he could see the play of muscles in her back through the thin fabric of his shirt, the flex in her arms.

As he'd hoped, the furthest island was free of all habitation, most paddle boarders and kayaks preferring to explore the cluster of islands nearer the jetty, moving from one to another, while the sail boats tended to head to the other end of the lake. He swung himself out of the kayak, extending a hand to Posy before pushing the small boat up onto the small beach.

'Our very own island,' Posy said appreciatively as she waded in. 'Shall we build a modest hut and live off coconuts and fish?'

'We'd soon starve. This is barely a hundred metres wide. One dwelling and a few fires and we'd be out of trees. Plus I hate to break it to you but there's a distinct lack of coconuts.'

'No coconuts? What will we do?'

'Luckily I am a trained hunter gatherer.' Nico reached into the kayak and retrieved the bag he had stuffed in at his feet. 'My lady, a feast awaits.'

It was hardly palace standard. No blanket or chairs, just the grainy sand to sit on. Bottled water and a grilled panini apiece stuffed with mozzarella, grilled vegetables and pesto. A dish of olives. But sitting there, the sun beating down overhead, feet in the warm water, Posy by his side, Nico felt something he hadn't felt in a very long time. He thought the word might be content.

CHAPTER ELEVEN

'You need a cause.'

Posy peered up at Melissa, the private secretary she was sharing with the Dowager Queen, and tried not to yawn. Last night Nico had kept his word and introduced her to Guido, Alessandro's partner. Usually on the nights she didn't have to endure the formal dinners, she ate in her rooms, either alone or with Nico, still struggling to come to terms with the knowledge she could order anything she liked whenever she liked and it would be prepared and delivered to her. She'd had a couple of useful conversations with the head chef and as a result he made sure he always stocked her favourite ingredients, creating delicious salads full of wild salmon, avocado, quinoa and all the other foods she filled up on to keep her body at optimum strength and fitness.

Of course now she could binge on pizza three times a day but old habits held hard. She might not be in class for eight hours but she stretched religiously and spent at least an hour on the old familiar exercises on the makeshift barre, in the centre, on pointe. She didn't ask herself why, didn't want to examine her motives too clearly, but she knew deep inside she hadn't quite given up on her dreams no matter what she told herself.

Last night had been the first time she had set foot in Nico's rooms. A similar size and layout to hers, they were decorated in a stark white and dark wood style, the furniture almost aggressively modern with its sharp lines and lack of decoration. He'd ordered a selection of the small tapas dishes so popular on the island, taking their influences from the cuisine of all the larger nations that had colonised it over the years, so plates of grilled vegetables, arancini, bruschetta, cheeses and rich meaty stews had all jostled for attention on the large glass table. Posy had warmed to Guido immediately and they had stayed up long into the night, drinking the rich red wine so typical of the island and eating until all they could do was lie supine and groan. He was a good conversationalist with a huge knowledge of the island's myths and traditions and, although Posy knew how hard it must be for him, to have no formal recognition as Alessandro's partner, no way to mourn publicly, he showed no bitterness or anger.

'They say,' he'd told her, 'that anyone who kisses under Neptune's Arch on the beach under the Villa Rosa will be in love for ever. Alessandro and I would sneak away there sometimes. It was a risk, a crazy risk but it was his way of committing to me. I knew what I was getting into, that we could never really be together, but I know he loved me and he knew how I felt. In the end that's all that matters.'

Posy hadn't been able to look at Nico as Guido had talked. They had kissed under Neptune's Arch—under it, against it, a lot more than kiss. But it hadn't been love that lured them there. 'We used to watch couples sneak onto the beach when I was a kid,' she'd admitted. 'It was a tradition for newly engaged couples to come out to the arch by night and kiss there to bring good luck to their lives together. Sofia always knew but she never tried to stop them. She was a big believer in love.'

What would she say if she knew Posy was even contemplating tying herself into a loveless marriage? She'd be horrified. She'd preferred to live alone and in love than settle for any of her wealthy, adoring admirers.

'Miss Marlowe?' Melissa's sharp voice brought Posy back to the far too early morning and she blinked, taking a long sip of her coffee as she did so. 'Yes. A cause. What do you mean?'

'It's the September Ball in two weeks.'

Posy nodded, holding onto her temper as best she could. She knew it was the ball in two weeks; after all, Melissa only mentioned it one hundred times a day.

'Your engagement will be announced along with an honorary title…'

'Hang on.' Posy held a hand up. 'A what?'

'An honorary title. It's customary when a Del

Castro marries a commoner...' she practically sniffed the last word '...that the said commoner is given a title until the wedding when they then assume their spouse's title. I believe you will become a Contessa.'

Posy swallowed a giggle. A *what*? 'Is that really necessary?' What would happen when she walked away? Would she get to keep the title, a unique souvenir of her engagement? She'd have to get a new passport; she'd bet that it would guarantee upgrades on every flight.

Melissa didn't see the joke. 'Yes. It's the custom. I told you.'

'Oh, well. If it's the custom.' Posy managed not to roll her eyes. There were many customs she was ignorant of and Melissa loved to enlighten her, whether it was the right way to wear her hair when she attended church in the royal pew or which pastry she should eat for breakfast on which saint's day.

'The King will announce your title and then you need to launch your cause, what you will be patron of. The Dowager Queen is patron of a literacy programme and the Queen a charity to alleviate child poverty on the island.'

Child poverty? Just a couple of the Queen's necklaces could probably solve that far better than a letterhead and a charity but Posy wasn't going to say that out loud. L'Isola dei Fiori was an island of contrasts, the two cities and many villages prosperous, as were many of the bigger farmers, but there were still far too many subsistence farmers eking out a meagre living from their small patches and the slum areas around the cities were as poor as any Posy had seen in places like Marseille or Naples. Nico was working hard to bring in the money to raise educational standards across the island and to introduce free health care but the old feudal systems were engrained and any change looked on with suspicion.

What on earth could Posy contribute—and what was the point if she wasn't staying?

'I'll think about it,' she said, but the doubts remained. She was twenty-four and all she knew was dance. She had no other skills.

The idea still preyed on her mind as she and

Nico returned from a date adorably riding adorable horses against an adorable backdrop of rolling hills and the sea. Luckily Posy's horse was both adorable and placid and when Nico put a steadying hand on her bridle it looked more lover-like than restraining. Horse-riding was one of the many things she had never learned to do for fear of injury and using the wrong muscles. And yes, she was enjoying these new outdoorsy skills, testing herself, her body. But, oh, how she missed the discipline of the studio.

Nico had been less talkative since their kayaking trip. It was as if having opened up once he was reluctant to do so again. On one hand Posy appreciated his return to polite and agreeable, it made her resolution not to continue this charade past the promised three months easier, but on the other it just reinforced how isolated she was in the palace, the disapproving Melissa her most constant companion. Guido could be a friend, but they would have to be circumspect. She didn't want to inadvertently betray his secrets with too close a friendship.

Usually she filled the silences with chatter. It was easier to talk inanely than to brood about her future and the opportunities she'd missed in the past, but today she couldn't put her lack of skills out of her mind. Obviously she wouldn't be here to figurehead a cause so it was all speculative anyway, but if she were here she wouldn't want to just hold meetings and fundraise, she'd want to be involved, properly hands-on. But how? What did she have to contribute?

'You're very quiet.'

'I thought you might appreciate the peace.'

He glanced over at her. 'Don't stop on my account. What's on your mind?'

Posy glared. 'Just because I'm quiet doesn't mean there's anything wrong.'

The corners of his mouth quirked into a smile. 'Maybe not but as you managed to talk while kayaking, while horse-riding, you even manage to make conversation with my aunt, it is out of character for you to sit worrying in silence.'

'I'm not worrying exactly,' she said with as much dignity as she could manage. 'I'm just won-

JESSICA GILMORE 209

dering what I'm good for. No, not that...' she scolded as his gaze automatically dropped to the vee in her dress. 'Eyes on the road, Your Royal Highness. I mean what could I be a patron of? I wouldn't want just a ceremonial title. If I'm to champion something I want to get stuck in.'

'Isn't it obvious? The arts.'

'Yes, but do you have any arts? I know there's folk dancing and folk songs, but beyond that? There's not even a theatre on the island, is there?'

'Not open. My great-grandfather—or was it my great-great-grandfather?—commissioned one. He was a great lover of the theatre—well, of actresses mainly, but it had the same result. But it closed down several years ago, longer maybe. It was mainly used by amateur groups and got too run down even for them.'

'Really? There's a theatre?' Posy was gripped by a homesickness so intense she clutched her stomach to try and stifle the pain. A stage, spotlights, curtains, wings. 'Can we visit it? Now?'

'Really? That's how you want to spend your first free afternoon in nearly three weeks?'

'Yes. Unless… You don't have to take me. You must have things you want to do. I'll see if one of the guards can, if that's okay, I mean. I won't be trespassing?'

'No, no, you won't be trespassing and, yes, I can take you. If that's what you really want to do.'

'It is,' Posy said, immeasurably cheered up by the prospect. 'I can't imagine anything else I'd rather do. I still don't see there's much scope to be a Patron of the Arts here but I always think best on stage. Maybe it'll spark a bright idea.'

It didn't take too long to get there. The theatre was near the centre of the island's capital, San Rocco, on a side street in a vibrant bohemian neighbourhood filled with cafés and restaurants, not far from the university. The front was boarded up but it wasn't hard for Posy to see the potential in the building. It had been built along art nouveaux lines, the lobby a graceful, marble introduction to the small but perfectly formed auditorium beyond, complete with stalls, a dress circle, upper circle and balcony. The royal box wasn't to one side as was usual but in the very centre of the dress circle, all the better for Nico's ancestor to watch the actresses and dancers from.

Posy stepped inside the auditorium, staring around in wonder, and took in a deep breath, regretting it almost immediately; it was very dusty. 'Look at this,' she managed, despite the dryness in her throat. 'It's perfect.'

Nico raised a sceptical brow. 'You are easily pleased. Dingy and in need of disinfecting, I would say.'

'It's not dingy,' she protested. 'It's full of character.' Okay, the velvet on the seats was threadbare, the great stage curtains were moth-eaten, the glass on the chandeliers smeared and dim. But the bones of the theatre were there. It wouldn't take a huge amount to clean it up and repair it. Possibly.

There were wooden steps at the end leading up to the stage. Posy walked up them carefully, feeling with her foot for any sign of rot or damp, anything that would make the stage unsafe, but it felt completely sound. 'I agree it's a little shabby,' she called down to Nico, who stood at the back of the stalls, watching her. 'But there doesn't seem to be anything structurally wrong. What a shame it hasn't been used for so long, you'd think someone would have tried to restore it.'

'It relied on royal patronage and neither my grandfather nor uncle cared for the theatre. The amateur groups kept it going for a while but when it started to need more than TLC they gave up too.'

'Poor old lady,' Posy murmured, and could have sworn the theatre answered her back with a dignified sniff.

She wandered into the wings and inhaled. No one had been here for a long, long time and yet she could still smell it, smell the anticipation, the sweat, the excitement. How many girls had stood here, stomachs tumbling with nerves, before stepping out onto that stage? How many times had she stood in the wings, rosin on her shoes, smile ready on her face, waiting for that moment when she ran onto the stage, doing the only thing that made her feel alive? How had she walked away from that?

She flexed a foot, pointing it instinctively, the stage calling to her louder and more enticing than a siren's song. It needed to be used, trodden upon, brought back to life. Before she could remember all the reasons this was a bad idea she pulled her phone out of her pocket and selected a piece of music, slipping off her shoes as she did so. The music would reach no further than her ears, she would be dancing barefooted in a fifties-style sundress but she had no choice. There was a stage and Posy had to dance.

She'd come home. The instant Nico had wrestled the last lock off the side door and ushered Posy inside she had changed, every atom in her alert, vibrant, positively buzzing with happiness. She didn't see a lobby caked in dirt, dust and graffiti; she saw a stately, welcoming space. To her the bar wasn't chipped and stained but ready and waiting for patrons to stand and drink. The seats weren't rusty and sagging but in need of some TLC, the chipped and faded plasterwork easy to fix with a coat of paint. Her smile grew wider with each step, her eyes brighter. This dark, dusty, cavernous space lifted her, sent her spinning with joy.

Literally.

The faintest strains of music reached him as Posy set her phone on the stage, a violin's melancholy note. She stood, leg pointed, arms raised, perfectly and utterly still. And then as the music swelled, as much as music played tinnily through a phone's speaker could swell, she began to dance. Nico stood, immobilised, as if each movement she made wound a spell around him, and one blink, one step would break the magic. He'd seen her move before, her prayer-like exercises, the arabesque on the beach, but he'd never seen her here in her natural environment.

As she danced the magic spread. He could see the seats as they should be, plush red velvet and filled with excited people, the chandelier gleaming, the freshly painted cherubs above blowing golden trumpets for eternity. And Posy herself: it was as if there were two, the girl in the pink dress, barefooted, hair flowing down her back, and the ballerina with her tight bun and layers of white tulle.

Nico had spent a lot of time in various theatres in various capital cities, watching various plays, ballets and operas. He had probably seen Posy dance before, sitting in a hospitality box in Covent Garden, taking no notice of the dark-haired girl in the Corps de Ballet, so used to watching genius at work he barely appreciated it any more. But not one of the exquisite performances he had watched moved him the way this dance did. She was music brought to life, a lyrical poem in motion, dancing for herself, for this old, forgotten theatre, for the life she had left behind.

He just couldn't understand why she had left it. He had loved his research, the logic mixed with experimentation, and had felt a pang when he had left it behind for the drier but eminently more sensible MBA. He was still interested in the subject matter, still read widely, still planned to lure the right people to the university, for his legacy to his island to be a healthy economy and a reputation as a market leader in using and developing clean energy. But he didn't yearn for research the way Posy yearned to dance. He'd always had a full and varied life whereas she was totally dedicated; nothing else really mattered. And he was no connoisseur but it seemed to him that the girl in front of him was full of life, burning with passion, every movement so evocative of loss and yearning it almost hurt to watch.

'I'm sorry, that was indulgent of me.'

He realised with a shock the music had stopped and Posy was standing at the edge of the stage, looking out at him. 'No, it was beautiful. What was it?'

'Giselle. I've danced it many times but always as a *willi*, a spirit. Never the title role. I always wanted to and here was my chance. The peasant girl saving the life of her Prince. I never thought I'd live it rather than dance it.'

'Live it? You plan to save me from being danced to my death by the ghosts of scorned women?'

'Maybe. It depends if you deserve saving or not. I was thinking more of the peasant girl and the Prince part rather than the whole supernatural and betrayal bit.'

'That's a relief. Is that the part you wanted to dance most?'

'Or Juliet.' She laughed, a little self-consciously. 'I always liked the really tragic roles best. But yes, it's a dancer's dream, to go from shy girl to falling in love to the whole mad scene at the end of Act One and then the tragically noble Act Two with that gorgeous *pas de deux*...not that it matters. That's not my role any more, not my life.'

No. She was quite clear about that. The thing Nico couldn't understand was why. Why if she danced like that?

Nico had to get married; he knew that. He knew that compatibility and respect were the best he could hope for and in the last few weeks he had believed it could actually happen; that he could marry someone he could be content with. He hadn't been able to believe his luck that he'd stumbled on her, on the safe partner he needed. With Posy there would be no huge dramas, no cold wars. She was diligent and disciplined, realistic and hardworking. She'd led a narrow life but she was intelligent and a quick learner, an easy conversationalist, good with people. Everything on his 'how to be a good queen' wish list personified with the added bonus of a sweet sensuality that heated his blood.

She deserved more than he could offer. Deserved more than life in a gilded cage. Deserved to dance the roles she craved. Deserved a man who loved her for all those qualities he had listed, not one who merely esteemed her for them.

She deserved better than him.

'You're right...'

He jumped as she came up beside him, wondering for one moment if he had spoken his thoughts aloud. 'I usually am.'

'You're going to make an insufferable king. But in this instance I'll let you have it. I should choose the arts. I should try and get enough money to restore this theatre and get touring companies to come here. That would be great for tourism but I'd want discounted tickets for locals and performances for schools. At the same time I could champion dance, music and drama for people of all ages.'

'That sounds like a great idea.'

'I don't really know how to go about it,' she confessed. 'But I know plenty of people who do. Maybe this is what I'm meant to do. If I can't dance myself I could inspire others to, show people how important music and drama and dance are.'

It was perfect. A working theatre with performances by some of Europe's touring groups would do wonders for tourism, offer visitors the culture they would expect when visiting a capital city. At the same time Posy's idea tied into his own plans to raise the level of education on the island, including more opportunities for adults. And if she was thinking so far ahead she must be considering staying past the end of their three-month agreement. Which was exactly what he wanted. Wasn't it?

CHAPTER TWELVE

WHEN POSY HAD been little and unable to decide what to do her mother had always made her write a list. 'You know the right path somewhere deep inside,' she would say. 'Write a list of fors and againsts and the right path will appear.' And it always had. Posy hadn't needed a list for a long, long time, her path had been so straightforward. Until it had suddenly twisted and the way she'd fled she'd chosen purely on instinct.

And look where instinct had brought her: away from her career, onto the front pages and about to get formally and possibly, probably, temporarily engaged to a man who didn't love her. Poised on the brink of, surreally, and hilariously, becoming a *Contessa* before—even more surreally—a princess. One day a queen.

Maybe. If she decided that was what she wanted.

She definitely needed a list.

Okay. Points in favour of staying: she would have a purpose. The idea of taking over the theatre and introducing an educational arts programme to L'Isola dei Fiori filled her with more excitement and hope than she would have believed possible a couple of months ago. She would be protected from the paparazzi, who currently had her firmly in their sights. She could make a life with Nico, whom she liked, whom she was attracted to, who seemed to like her. Who needed her...

Posy closed her eyes. Needed her for *what*? To provide romantic photos and lure the tourists in? To act as a hostess? To provide him with heirs? None of that was something only she could do. Nico didn't need *her*, he needed a wife, any wife.

Okay. That was the first item on the 'against' list. What else? When she'd walked away she had thought she would probably never dance again but marrying Nico would ensure that actually happened. Had she really given up on her dream?

She would live her whole life in the spotlight. Nico didn't love her...

Posy's stomach twisted. It wasn't as if she were actually looking for love, but neither had she consciously *not* been looking for it. She was only twenty-four. Was she ready to give up any chance of really falling for someone? Of someone really falling for her?

It was hard to imagine settling right now when she was surrounded by so much loved-upness it almost made her ill. Thanks to a sterling effort by some of the palace staff enough of the rooms in Villa Rosa were both clean and secure enough for her whole family to stay there and Posy had moved back in yesterday to welcome them to her home for the last time. It had been an emotional reunion, even though it wasn't that long since they'd last all gathered together here at the villa for Immi and Matt's engagement celebration barely two months before, but knowing it was the last time they would be able to call it their second home had provoked more than a few nostalgic tears.

'After all,' Miranda had said, hand in hand with her new husband, Cleve, 'the villa was a refuge when we needed it. It brought us love and happiness. It seems right to share that with others but it won't be the same. Not for us.'

It was as if they all had agreed to make the most of this last stay. The summer hadn't yet broken and so the family had spent the day swimming and sunbathing, wandering along the cliff tops and revisiting their favourite haunts in the villa for a nostalgic wallow.

The evening had drawn in and, after a feast sent over by the palace chefs, they were all relaxing in the sitting room separated into pairs, apart from Posy all alone in the love seat. She couldn't help a sad, wistful sigh for when they had been a family of six, not nine. It wasn't that she didn't like her sisters' various husbands and fiancés, she really did, it was just they were their own families now. Little complete units of two—soon to be three in Miranda's case. Everything had changed irrevocably. For her as much as any of them.

'Why so sad, Rosy-Posy?' Her parents were just as bad as her sisters, curled up together on the sofa, actually holding hands. At their age! This year out had brought them closer together than ever. Not that Posy was complaining. After several weeks of watching Nico's uncle and aunt ignore each other it was lovely to be back in her parents' all-encompassing loving circle.

'I'm not sad. I'm thinking.'

'That explains it, then.'

'Careful, Posy, you'll hurt your brain.'

Miranda and Imogen were sitting at opposite ends of the room, Andie lying next to Cleve as he absent-mindedly massaged her growing tummy, Immi and Matt cuddling up together on the window seat, but her twin sisters still managed to insult her in unison. Maybe nothing too much had changed after all.

The only person not to smile at their joint offensive was Portia, who looked penetratingly at Posy. The sole member of the family who knew the truth, she'd been trying to get Posy alone all day—and Posy had eluded her at every turn. She didn't know why; it should have been a relief to stop acting the happy bride-to-be for one moment, to stop laughing good-naturedly at all the Princess Posy jokes, to allow herself to drop her guard. But she was more than a little scared that if she stopped pretending even for a minute she wouldn't be able to carry on at all. And it was lovely seeing her parents so happy and proud, so relaxed, the last thing she wanted was to be the person to change that.

'Isn't Nico joining us?' Javier, Portia's handsome film-star husband, asked.

'Yes, when am I going to meet my future son-in-law?' her father chimed in. Posy had dreaded seeing her parents, knowing that they had seen the pictures of her and Nico, but they had fallen over themselves to reassure her of their support. Her father had made it clear that he blamed Nico entirely for the whole fiasco. Posy hadn't known whether to be relieved or not when Immi had loyally pointed out it was the photographer at fault, leading Portia to defend the freedom of the press, and the whole discussion had become a heated one about body shaming and double standards. Normally she would have loved to join in the debate but today she'd sat quietly, all too aware the body that had been shamed was hers.

'We're not actually officially engaged, Dad, and you'll meet him tomorrow,' she answered, feeling Portia's investigative gaze on her. 'Before the ball. I wanted you all to myself tonight.'

'What's he like?' her mother asked. 'You know him, don't you, Javier? Is he good enough for Posy?'

'You thought so when you introduced us,' Posy said meaningfully in case Javier had forgotten the story he and Nico had concocted.

Javier smiled at her reassuringly. 'I was a couple of years older than Nico when I lived here, so I didn't see much of him outside of lessons. I was always friendlier with Alessandro. Nico had a reputation as a wild boy, he hated the restrictions of the palace, but he's grown up to be a steady young man. He cares a great deal about L'Isola dei Fiori's future and how to ensure it thrives.'

'It's Posy's future I'm concerned with,' her father growled and Posy was overcome with a rush of love for her parents, who had always supported her, even when they didn't understand her. 'I hate that you've given up ballet, Posy. Why the rush to marry? Can't you wait a couple of years?'

'Nico needs to take on his duties here now, Daddy. He had a couple of years after Alessandro's death to take his MBA so he could help manage the economy with confidence, but he can't put off joining the government any longer. And I need to be with him, helping him. I'm looking at ways to make dance part of my life here.'

'That's all very well and good but what's he like as a person, not a prince? What do you love about him, Posy?' Since when had her sensible and capable mother got so romantic?

'Yes.' Miranda shifted with an audible huff, her hands automatically moving to cradle her stomach. 'Tell us about him. He must be pretty special to lure you away from the stage.'

Posy stared at her family, searching for the right

words to convince them. 'Erm… Well. He's really handsome…'

The twins immediately made gagging noises and Posy threw a pillow in Imogen's direction, remembering in time that Miranda's pregnancy gave her immunity and contenting herself with glaring instead. 'He is. He's always winning Europe's Hottest Prince in *HRH Magazine*'s polls. His eyes are the darkest blue I've ever seen and when he smiles it's like you're the only person he sees…' Where had that come from? She shifted, picking up another cushion to cuddle and hide her embarrassment behind as her mother heaved a romantic sigh.

Better stop dwelling on his looks before she moved on to his shoulders and forearms and hands… 'He's clever. Properly clever. He was studying for a PhD in some kind of engineering and then switched to an MBA when Alessandro died. He loves being active. He finds it hard, palace life, because he really likes being outdoors pushing himself. Rock climbing and skiing and things like that.'

'Impressive CV, Posy, but beyond the hot body, action-man hobbies and big brains what's he really like? What made you fall for him?' Imogen laid a hand on Matt's knee and smiled up at him. 'Apart from the title, that is.'

Posy glared, needled by her sister's words. 'There's lots of things, actually. He has this absolutely huge sense of duty. I mean, people don't see that, they see the motorboats and the girls and the parties and the rest but he's always put the island first—that's why he switched to an MBA. He knew he couldn't govern the island without that kind of knowledge. He has such big plans. He wants to make L'Isola dei Fiori a tourist paradise while keeping the heart of it intact, to improve the health and education for everyone, to expand the university to make it a world leader in technology, especially renewables. And he's loyal. He doesn't let many people in but if he's on your side he'll defend you to the end, do anything to protect you.' As he was protecting her with the best weapon he had—his name. 'He's thoughtful and really kind. He carries the world on his shoulders but pretends it doesn't weigh anything. He's the best person I know and that's why I'm marrying him,' she finished defiantly.

There was a moment's silence. Posy's whole family were staring at her.

'I can't wait to meet him, darling,' her mother said at last and the others chimed in. All except Portia, whose expression was troubled.

Posy hugged the cushion tighter. Where had all that come from, that torrent of words? Of emotions? Worst of all she'd meant every word.

Did she feel like that because she had spent so much of the last few weeks with Nico? Was it simply Stockholm Syndrome? Or was it the sex twisting her brains and emotions with all those feel-good hormones?

Or was she actually falling for Nico? And if so what on earth was she going to do when he'd made it all too clear that emotions weren't part of their deal at all?

It should have been a relief, this small respite from looking after Posy. Nico had never appreciated before how difficult life in the palace could be for someone not bred for it. Not only did Posy not know her way around, not know the customs or etiquette, she didn't speak the language. Nor did she have any friends or acquaintances on the island. Oh, she had bodyguards, tutors, maids and the private secretary she still shared with his aunt, but otherwise she was completely dependent on him.

He had obviously anticipated spending some time with his chosen bride aside from the official 'dates'—he wanted his marriage to work as some kind of partnership, after all. He just hadn't expected to spend *this* much time, to find himself so responsible for another human being.

Nor had he expected to find it so easy.

Nico paced around his sitting room. Soon he would have to steel himself to move into the much larger suite traditionally lived in by the heir and his family. Alessandro had lived in all those rooms alone, never changing the décor chosen for him when he was twenty-one, décor that represented the man the palace wanted Alessandro to be, not the man he actually was. Nico intended to give Posy free rein to redecorate the rooms any way she saw fit, to give her one piece of this old, formal place that could really be hers. Would that be enough to keep her, a place of her own?

He turned and looked at his sitting room. He'd only been here a few weeks so it wasn't that surprising that, although it had been furnished with his own furniture, shipped over from Boston, he hadn't personalised any of his suite yet. There were no books on the dark wooden shelves, no pictures on the white walls. But then there hadn't been a great deal of personal stuff in the Boston apartment either and he'd lived there for five years. He had one photo of Alessandro, a candid shot of his cousin out on a boat, laughing as the spray hit him, on his desk but he displayed no pictures of his grandparents or his parents. No ex-girlfriend special enough to deserve a lasting place anywhere—no ex-girlfriend special enough to deserve a temporary place. He didn't buy art or ceramics or anything that showed his personal taste and all his books were textbooks, his magazines research journals and he read most of those electronically anyway.

By contrast Posy had already personalised her rooms with little more than a sprinkle of fairy dust. She'd arrived on the island with a backpack and a small holdall and half of her things were still at the villa and yet photographs of her whole family—and a much-loved and deceased golden retriever—sat on her bedside table. Books and magazines were strewn across her coffee table and haphazardly piled onto her bookshelves. She had raided some of the unused rooms so that cushions were piled high on all seating and lamps cast warm glows from every nook. Her sewing basket sat on the floor, usually open with a pair of unfinished shoes on top—what she planned to do with all the darned pointe shoes once she'd worked her way through the box, he wasn't quite sure. She collected gifts and souvenirs every-where they went and examples of the lacework, pottery and glass ornaments presented to her as they toured the island were proudly displayed on every available surface. She'd kept the vases filled with flowers and added glass bowls with pebbles and shells she'd collected, and scarves and throws decorated every chair. The main rooms of the various royal suites were large affairs, acting as sitting/dining rooms informally and private reception rooms more formally, big enough for small parties. They were grand, purposefully so, luxurious but not usually cosy. Somehow Posy had made hers so. Made herself a home even if it was temporary, something Nico had never really had.

He'd grown up here, son of the second son, a spare whose use was supposed to be temporary. No one wanted a spare to feel too much at home in a place where they had no real purpose, just a drain on the royal purse. He'd liked Boston a lot but that had never been home either, the city so busy, the winters so very cold and long. He'd always intended to return to L'Isola dei Fiori armed with a purpose, with a way to make his own life, one away from the palace. Then he might have thought about putting down roots, buying some art, a photograph or two. Maybe.

He'd never envisioned anyone else living with him. Never met anyone who might have persuaded him otherwise, anyone he could have trusted. Maybe he'd been looking in all the wrong places. Maybe it was easier to look in the wrong places and know he'd be disappointed than look elsewhere and risk actually being really hurt. Maybe.

Damn but it was quiet. He'd been looking forward to the peace but the quiet just seemed eerie, his bed too big, his rooms too stark, every meeting duller than the one before.

He was relieved when the shrill ringtone interrupted his introspective pacing and he was conscious of a lightening of mood when he saw Posy's name lit up on his phone's screen. Unwilling—or unable—to analyse why that might be, he snapped, far more curtly than he intended, 'Yes?'

'Oh, hi, Nico.' He'd thrown her, he could tell. 'Is this a bad time?'

'No.' He tried to soften his tone, aware that his irritation with her was completely irrational.

Why did she have to be so damn reasonable? 'It's fine.'

'Oh, okay. It's good news. You know I emailed Bruno, my old ballet master, to see if he could put me in touch with some people to advise me on the best way to go about starting the Arts programme? Well, he's come here. For the ball. And he's brought some third-year students to perform as well. Isn't that amazing?'

'He's just turned up here with some students?'

'Well, no, not exactly. I mean, I invited him. They like to give the third years performing opportunities but it was such short notice and he's so busy, I didn't think for a moment he'd actually come.' Posy was breathless, the words tumbling out of her in her excitement. This man, Bruno, clearly meant a lot to her. Nico was conscious of a tension in his shoulders, his grip on his phone too tight. 'He knows everyone, from philanthropists to musicians, and does loads of educational work on the side. If he's willing to advise me then I'm so less likely to make mistakes.'

'That's great.' It was. Posy was clearly fired up

about restoring the theatre, which meant she was likely to want to see the project through. Not that she actually needed to be married to him to accomplish that. 'Is there time for them to perform tonight? My aunt has spent a lot of time putting the timings together.' He had no idea why he was being so dampening, why Posy's news was sending out danger alerts when it all seemed so possible.

'She's delighted. I've never heard her sound so pleased. She actually called me Rosalind rather than Miss Marlowe, which is a major step forward, I reckon. There's loads of space in the ballroom, enough for an entire company, not just a quartet. I thought you'd be pleased.'

'I am. It's great, well done.' He tried to muster some enthusiasm into his voice, aware he was overdoing it and sounding more like a children's entertainer. 'Are you planning to show him the theatre tomorrow?'

'He has to get straight back to class so there isn't time. We're popping over there now and then straight back to the palace for rehearsals. There's just about time.'

'You're cutting it fine.' He glanced at his watch. Two p.m. 'The ball starts in six hours. Don't you have to get ready?' His mother and aunt usually started getting ready around lunchtime for the September Ball, massages and manicures, hair-dressers and facials.

Posy laughed. 'There's six hours yet. It'll take me twenty minutes. Actually, make that forty if I have a quick shower. I'm used to dressing up, remember? That's why you've hired me.'

She was joking but her words twisted in his gut all the same. He had hired her, hired, bribed, persuaded—the word didn't matter—to do a job. And it was a huge job. She was only twenty-four, her whole life still ahead of her. Did she really want to limit herself to this narrow life on a small island? Was he really willing to allow her?

'Forty minutes? It'll take me longer than that.' He tried to inject some humour into the conversation. 'So you're heading to the theatre now?'

'That's why I'm calling. Do you want to meet

us there, meet Bruno and explain some of the history of the theatre to him?'

'That sounds great but I can't, meetings, you know.'

'Of course, I should have thought. I'll see you later, at the reception. My family's looking forward to seeing you. I think they were hoping you'd have had time to make it over to the villa. I warned them how busy you are but they never listen to me, perils of being the youngest.'

Was that hurt he could detect in her voice? He had meant to visit the villa yesterday to welcome the Marlowes to the island—and to formally ask Mr Marlowe for Posy's hand, despite Posy's cross reminder that she was a grown woman and quite able to speak for herself. But he'd known how much Posy was looking forward to having all her family around her, to being just a Marlowe girl again, not a Prince's paramour or a tabloid sensation, and he hadn't been able to bring himself to intrude.

Plus he didn't know how to be part of a big,

cosy family and he'd had enough of being the outsider. 'I'm sorry, it's been so busy.'

'No, it's fine, don't worry. I guess I'll see you at the reception.' There was a wistful question in her voice, which Nico ignored.

'See you then. Enjoy the theatre.'

He put the phone down and stared unseeingly at the white walls, the wistful sound in Posy's voice still echoing in his ears. He'd known her five weeks. Just five weeks. And already she needed more than he could give her; she'd probably deny it, even believe her own words, but he knew.

He just didn't know what he was going to do about it.

CHAPTER THIRTEEN

'I STILL CAN'T believe they were just left here to stand empty.' Bruno, the Ballet Company's irascible ballet master, stood, hands on hips, and looked disbelievingly at the studio. Posy had already toured him through the theatre itself and onto the stage before showing him the maze of backstage rooms she had discovered: offices, dressing rooms, rehearsal spaces and, best of all, two huge studios, barres and mirrors still in place, the floor perfectly sprung.

'They were filthy,' she said. 'But I had them cleaned up and I've been using them for exercises. It's not far from the palace and, although there's a gym there I can use, this floor is just so much better. The only problem is the temperature. It's still warm enough, just, but give it a few more weeks and it won't be any good for my muscles, far too cold. But there's so much to do here, fussing about heating in here feels silly.'

Bruno nodded. He didn't ask why a future princess, a girl who had given up dance, needed a professional studio at the right temperature and Posy knew she wouldn't have had an answer for him. Just as she didn't know why she had put all her energies over the last couple of weeks into cleaning up the studios rather than the offices or something else more practical. Why she darned so many shoes. Why she put herself through a class every day, even though there was no teacher, no other students, just the music and the comforting repetition of barre and centre work.

'So, I was thinking it seems a shame to waste this gorgeous space.'

His eyebrows snapped together. 'You want to set up a ballet company?'

'No.' She paused, momentarily seduced by the idea before dismissing it. 'No, L'Isola dei Fiori is far too small to sustain one, I think if we could attract some of the better touring companies we'll be doing well. Besides, a theatre like this needs variety: plays, operas, concerts. It's the only way to make it viable. No, I was thinking summer retreats for professional dancers and summer schools for children. It ties perfectly in with Nico's tourism idea—the whole family could come here for a holiday, drop aspiring ballet-mad child here for the day and they can go off and explore the island knowing they're leaving their child in expert hands.'

'Your hands? I always thought you'd make an excellent teacher.'

Ouch. It was a compliment but it stung harder than his harshest critique. What did they say? Those who could do...she'd always thought she could.

'No, not me. I won't be able to train or get the experience needed in time. To get the right kids—and the right fees—I'll need high-calibre teachers with workshops from some of the big names. Workshops from people like you, from some of the soloists, not just ours—yours—but from Paris, Rome, a really international school appealing to an international audience. Realistically we're more likely to attract Italian tourists, maybe Spanish and French, than people from the UK so we need to cater for that.'

'And this will fulfil you?' Bruno's eyes fixed on her, the exact same expression on his face as when he focused on a poorly turned-out foot. 'Organising summer schools, fundraising for the theatre, getting the arts into schools here? This is how you see your life now?'

Posy turned away so he couldn't see the yearning on her face. 'No one can dance for ever, Bruno. We all need a retirement plan. And you just said I'd make a good teacher. This is an extension of that.'

'One day you'll make a great teacher. Not now. You're twenty-four, Posy. You have your entire career before you. Don't you remember when you were in Year Three and I brought you to dance an exhibition, just like those children out there are doing?' He waved a hand in the direction of the other studio where the four young dancers were practising for the evening. 'That was... what? Five years ago? I promoted you and Daria straight into the Company that week. How can you walk away?'

Posy swallowed. She couldn't admit to him that she'd eavesdropped, overheard his damning words. He saw the Company as a whole, wouldn't understand her motives, would think she'd walked away because of a selfish need to shine. Right now, back in the studio, still sweating from the class he'd taught, she didn't understand her reasons either. 'Life has changed for me, Bruno.'

'Is he worth it? Your Prince?'

'I think so.' She pushed Nico's brusqueness earlier out of her mind. He must be stressed with the big announcement later, the prospect of meeting her entire family. She knew how he felt. Every time she thought of the all too public engagement announcement she felt nauseous, like stage nerves amplified one hundred times.

It didn't help that she hadn't slept last night, her mind a whirling mass of confused thoughts, all of them centred on Nico. On the things she'd said to her family about him. Trying to analyse her feelings until she was almost crying in frustration. One thing was all too clear: she was in too deep now to just walk away. Her life was more and more embedded here on the island. Maybe she should just accept the inevitable and admit she was planning to stay. That it made sense on many levels: she'd be protected; she'd have a purpose, a role she could really get excited about. The only real problem was Nico himself. Because if she *was* developing real feelings for him…

If? Funny how she still tried to fool herself. But how could she really admit there was no 'if' about it? Maybe it was a good thing he'd been so offhand earlier. She'd missed him so much, had been so relieved to hear his voice that she'd been on the verge of telling him she didn't need the three-month grace period, that she was in. That she had a purpose here—and she wasn't sure she could walk away from him either. No, she couldn't tell him the last part. Not yet. It wasn't part of their agreement, after all. One step at a time.

'So what are you dancing this evening? We

have time for some coaching. You still represent us, Posy, whether you wish to or not.'

'Me?' She turned in surprise. 'I'm not...'

'Of course you are. You want to launch this scheme, then you need to show why it's important. What will it be?'

Posy stood stock-still. For the last five years of her life she had wanted this man to single her out for a solo. And now he had it was the wrong time, the wrong place, the wrong reason and simply too damn late for her.

'I hadn't thought there would be any need to.'

'Well, think now. Quick, we don't have much time.'

There was only one real answer. 'Juliet?'

He nodded. 'Yes. Do you have the music?'

She always had the music. The studio didn't have a working sound system but she'd brought in some speakers and so she slotted in her phone and pulled her shoes out of her bag, glad that she'd joined in with the class Bruno had just conducted for his students. She was warmed up and supple, even if she had only been managing an hour, two hours tops, over the last few weeks rather than the eight hours she really needed to meet Bruno's standards.

She finished tying the ribbons on her pointe shoes, took a deep breath and took her position in the middle of the studio. She was Juliet, young, at a ball in her honour, her life before her. She could do this...

Nico froze. The studios had long viewing windows and so, from the dark, dingy passageway, he could see everything inside them both. In the first studio two serious-looking young men and two equally serious-looking young women were painstakingly going over and over a short routine. There was nothing glamorous about the loose buns, legwarmers and battered shoes; this was very clearly work.

As was the scene in the next studio. Posy was also wearing a leotard. She had paired hers with a long wrap skirt, her hair bundled up so the nape of her neck, her shoulders were clearly visible. She looked delicate, like a wisp—or she would have done if it weren't for the play of muscles in her legs, her back. There was a lot of power in that slim build. She was listening intently to a whippet-thin man, probably in his early fifties, who gesticulated a lot as he talked, pausing to demonstrate a move, a pose. Nico froze when the man held Posy, manipulating her into place. *His* territory, his body whispered, *his.*

'Once more,' the man said. 'You're fourteen, remember? Filled with anticipation, with happiness. Now go...'

She nodded, took up a pose—and then as the music started she began to move. Nico had seen her dance before, on the beach and on the stage, but here she was in the studio, her natural element, up on the tips of her toes, the blunt edge of her shoes making her look as if she were floating, balancing on the merest edge and yet able to make it look effortless. He stayed stock-still, watching until she finally spun to a stop and held her pose. It looked so easy somehow and yet her skin shone with perspiration and her chest heaved with exertion. But she was grinning, clearly as exhilarated as he was after a long mountain-bike ride, after scaling a sheer rock face or riding the rapids. All things he could no longer do. Had she felt as caged as he, without her usual outlet? More so, he suspected. Dancing wasn't just her pastime; it was her entire life. She'd tried to explain but he'd never understood before.

Now he understood all too well.

'Yes, that's it,' the man said. 'I don't know what's happened to you, Posy. You're a little out of practice and your technique isn't quite as spot on as usual, all of which is to be expected after a break of a few weeks…but there's a quality to your dancing, Posy, a poignancy, a maturity I have never seen before. A fire.'

Posy hadn't moved but Nico could tell she was struggling to contain herself, to keep that poise she prized herself on. The poise he prized in her. The poise that made her such a perfect choice to be his bride. 'Thank you, Bruno. From you that means everything.'

Everything. Such telling words. Nico swallowed hard. His chest seemed to have petrified, his heart heavy within it. He hadn't felt this kind of physical emotional pain since, well, since he was sixteen and found himself a front-page laughing stock. Only that had been a deliberate betrayal. This wasn't a betrayal at all, just a realisation…

No. He'd known all along that Posy wasn't for the island. Wasn't for him. She'd played her part brilliantly, was prepared to carry on playing it.

The question was for how long—and how long would he let her?

Bruno's voice brought Nico back to the here and now. 'Look, Posy. I know you have left us but I meant it when I said the door was open for you to return at any time. I admit, I saw a role for you as *coryphée*, maybe as an assistant to me one day, but if you dance with the emotion I saw just now? Then there may be another role for you. No one knows yet but Isabella is pregnant. She'll be cutting down on her work soon and that leaves a space for a soloist. I don't see why that couldn't be you. Why you couldn't get that chance to prove yourself.'

Posy froze, her eyes wide with hope. 'A soloist? Me?'

'You should have been there years ago but somehow you never quite made that leap. Now may be your time. You're finally ready if you want it enough. I can keep that door open for you for three weeks at the very most but I'll need a decision by then. Earlier if possible. I'm sure your Prince is very nice but you can marry any time. You can't say the same about dance. Think about it.'

'I will.'

Just two words. But as she said them Nico realised with a physical pain that he hadn't managed to encase his heart in stone at all and somehow, without his even being aware, Posy had snuck in through his defences and lodged herself there. Which put him in the uncomfortable situation of doing the right thing.

Nico turned and walked away. He had some thinking to do but he already knew what his decision would be.

'Hello, stranger.' Posy turned and smiled shyly at Nico as he walked into her room. 'Are you ready for tonight?'

Nico's hand brushed his pocket, feeling the solid bulk of the two boxes he had concealed in there; the larger held a diamond necklace, begrudgingly unearthed from the vault by his aunt, who didn't see why, just because there was going to be a new Crown Princess, she should give up the heirlooms she had enjoyed for years—no matter that, as Queen, she had access to plenty more.

The other held a ring. Not an heirloom, a diamond flanked by two sapphires the colour of the sea. A ring he had bought himself, knowing it was perfect for her. All he had to do was give it to her.

The box was leather, lined with satin, and yet it weighed him down as if it were lead.

'As ready as I'll ever be. You look beautiful, like a prima ballerina.'

'Thank you. Luckily I had already chosen this dress so no costume changes needed.' She had opted for a simple cream gown, ballerina style, fitted to just below her breasts the skirt falling softly to mid-calf length. The cream was shot through with gold thread so she shimmered as she walked. She'd pulled her hair back, a heavy dark coil on top of her head, wrapped around with gold thread. Small cream and gold pins twisted in the shining mass.

'You're looking forward to dancing?'

'It's a dream come true. I know it's not a full-length ballet and I'm in the middle of the ballroom, not on a stage, but I'm finally dancing Juliet in front of an audience. Everything I've spent my life working for is happening right here. I'm equally thrilled and terrified but I'm ready for this. I've been ready for a long time.'

'Yes,' he said heavily. 'You deserve it.'

She turned then, concern on her face. 'Are you okay? You've been, I don't know, maybe a little preoccupied all day. Can I help?'

He took a deep breath. It was time. 'Posy, remember when you agreed to help me out?'

'Agreed to...you mean the relationship?' Her eyes were wary. She knew something was up.

'Yes. You agreed to three months before deciding either way. Time enough to showcase the island and to get the press to change the story. To give you time to work out whether you could live this life and figure out an alternative if not.'

'I did, but...'

'It's unfortunate that the September Ball is halfway through that three months, unfortunate that my uncle wants our engagement announced tonight. An engagement is a bigger thing than a love affair, especially when it's an engagement to a Crown Prince. Ending a relationship is one thing but an engagement is quite another. It could cause quite a scandal, reignite interest in you.'

'I hadn't thought of that. You're probably right. But...'

'Remember what you said that afternoon, when I offered you a three-month trial and said you could walk away at the end? You said I could do the same, if I wanted to. You gave me the same get-out clause. Told me that if this wasn't right for me then I needed to let you know, that you wouldn't hold me to this engagement.'

Her eyes widened but she tilted her chin so she was looking right at him, as if she could see into the heart of him. But she couldn't; he'd made sure of that. 'Say the words, Nico.'

'I'm invoking that clause, Posy. I don't think we should get married and I won't be announcing our engagement tonight. You're free.'

'I see…' she said tonelessly. She was the same girl in the same dress but it was as if all the light had gone out of her.

'It's not you…'

She stepped back at that, colour high in her cheeks. 'You don't need to say it, Nico. This isn't some grand love affair—you don't have to worry about my feelings. Of course it's me. You don't care who you marry as long as she looks right and acts right and isn't as emotional as your mother or as cold as your aunt and needs nothing from you but is prepared to pretend she adores you and bears your children. Right? So I must be failing in one of those criteria, which means it is very much me.'

His hand fell to the ring box again. 'I thought you'd be relieved.'

'When my whole family is here expecting me

to announce my engagement? The palace is full of people expecting it! I didn't used to care what people think but turns out, after being plastered over the front pages, I'm a little more sensitive than I realised. I don't want people to gossip about me any more.'

Of course. The only reason she'd agreed to this whole engagement was because of the gossip—that and because she had no idea what to do with her life. One of those things was solved; he would take care of the other. 'I'll tell your family we are taking things slowly, that although we're still secretly engaged, in light of your promotion at work we've decided not to make it public yet to give you time to return to London for a few months. I'll let my family know the same thing. We'll then announce your appointment as Patron of the Arts, starting with your intention to renovate the theatre and introduce a programme into schools—we'll make sure everyone goes away thinking that's the announcement planned for tonight.'

'So I won't be a Contessa after all? I can't say

I'm sorry, although I was looking forward to being upgraded on flights.' She was trying to smile but her mouth trembled and Nico had to take a step back to stop himself from kissing her until she trembled for a whole other reason. 'Then what? I just walk away?'

If only it were that easy. He needed a clean break but he had to think of her and the best way to manage her exit strategy. Somehow it was easier if he coated it in business speak. 'I'm sorry but I think we need to carry on this charade for a while longer.' It took everything he had to keep looking her full in the face, to keep his voice casual, even a little bored. 'It would be great if you do actually take on the patron role for real. You have a platform now. It would be a shame to waste it. If you could come over a few times to work on that and the tourism project…'

'So that's what we're calling it now? You mean being photographed with you? Pretending we're together.'

'Yes, and I'll come to London. And then next spring we can issue a press release saying we've drifted apart. Perils of a long-distance relationship.'

'Meanwhile you've perused your grandmother's dossier and picked out the perfect bride.'

There was no sugar-coating his answer. 'Yes.'

'I see. You have it all worked out.'

'Posy. I am really grateful—'

'The villa,' she cut him off. 'You still need it, I suppose?'

'Can you afford to keep it?'

Her eyes glinted then, defiant. 'No, but Javier could without even noticing the cost. He loves it too. I could sell it to him.'

A wave of tiredness swept over Nico. That ridiculous pink villa. If he hadn't been drawn there, hadn't thought it would make the perfect hotel, then they wouldn't be standing here now, staring at each other over a newly opened chasm with no way across. And sure, he had been the one to shake the ground but it didn't make any of this easier. Not that Posy could suspect that. He knew her all too well. If she suspected for one moment he wasn't for real, if she had any idea that he…that he loved her, goddammit…then she would insist on staying, Throw her one chance away out of misguided loyalty and an overdeveloped sense of honour. Out of pity.

Would it make any difference if she did love him back? No. Giving up on a dream was an awful lot to ask of another human being. He would never be worth that kind of sacrifice.

'Do what you want. I'll give you fair market price.'

She sagged then, defeated, just for a moment but it was enough. 'Fine, have it. I'll talk to my solicitor.'

'Good. Posy, this is for the best. You're meant for the stage, for dance. You need to go back to London and shine, not spend your life here shouldering burdens that were never yours to shoulder.'

She straightened and turned away to gaze out of the window. 'You may be right. Nico, I need a moment. I'll meet you downstairs.'

It was his turn to pause before bowing and turning away, the ring box still weighing him down, taunting him with its forbidden promise. But he knew with utter certainty it was the right thing to do. Better end it now rather than in a couple of months when letting her go would hurt more and she'd lost her chance at the promotion. Better let her go now than marry her and watch her regret her choice more every passing day. He hadn't done the right thing for Alessandro and he regretted it every single day. Hated himself for being too selfish to free Alessandro to live his life. But he could free Posy. And maybe one day, when it stopped hurting, he'd know that he'd done a really noble thing for once in his life.

CHAPTER FOURTEEN

POSY STARED AT her hands and tried to formulate a coherent thought, a way of framing what had just happened, but the words slipped out of reach. Last night she had come to a realisation, this morning a decision. And sure, Bruno's offer had thrown her, seduced her because she would always, *always* be a ballerina, but the last few weeks had shown her the possibility of a different kind of life. Not a normal life, sure, not a free one, but a life with purpose.

It wasn't an easy life. She didn't like the stuffy traditions and frosty atmosphere and customs and bodyguards and the press following her everywhere she went. But she liked it when Nico smiled with those navy-blue eyes and she knew he had her back, when he grazed her arm with the back of his hand and she trembled with sheer lust.

She liked it when he noticed she was uncomfortable, whether she was trapped in a dull conversation or out of her depth socially, and he came to her rescue so smoothly no one noticed. She still had his shirt, hidden in her wardrobe, crumpled and unwashed, smelling of him, a reminder of when he had understood her, protected her.

And it wasn't one-sided. He confided in her, relaxed with her; she knew he let down some of his defences with her. She'd felt needed. More fool her.

Sure she'd missed dancing, was lost without the ritual of it, but the theatre was a way of combining old Posy and new Princess Rosalind and changing lives for the better. There was no denying she'd have liked her Odette/Odile moment first but she was ready to choose a new path.

But Nico didn't want her to. He wanted her to return to London with Bruno and take the promotion, and of course he was right but...

He wanted her to take the promotion.

She hadn't *mentioned* the promotion.

So how did he know?

The only other person who knew about the offer was Bruno and he was busy putting his hapless students through their paces until they were perfect—and even if Nico had bumped into Bruno she couldn't imagine Bruno saying anything. It simply wasn't his style.

But hadn't she asked Nico to come to the theatre? What if he had? What if he'd overheard her conversation with Bruno?

Or maybe she was delusional, clinging onto some ridiculous hope. He'd made it clear: her usefulness was at an end, her exit planned. And she would walk away with a promotion and money in her pocket. Things actually were going to work out for her. It almost seemed too good to be true…

Selling Villa Rosa would enable her to buy a small flat in London, the promotion would mean more money plus more teaching and sponsorship opportunities. She'd be a fool to not grab this chance with both hands. Who knew? Maybe in ten, twenty years' time she'd look back at this interlude with nostalgia, her few weeks of being an almost-princess. Maybe she'd see pictures of Nico in the papers and tell her children about her romance with a prince, her very own fairy tale.

Only this wasn't a fairy tale and Nico was no Prince Charming. She didn't love him because he was perfect—she loved him because he wasn't.

Posy turned and looked at the rooms; somehow they had come to feel like home. She still felt a little uncomfortable when she came in to find her bed made, her bathroom cleaned and her laundry miraculously done and she wasn't sure she'd ever get used to being tailed by two six-foot-something unsmiling men in dark suits, but she loved the old palace with its maze of corridors and twisty staircases. Her Italian was coming on and she only unknowingly ignored some archaic custom three times a day now, rather than ten or twenty.

And Nico was here.

Would he tell his perfect princess bride about Alessandro? Would he host small, intimate dinners with his bride and Guido where all etiquette was cast aside and they acted like the family they so very nearly were? Would he take his bride kayaking away from the bodyguards and onlookers, buy her a picnic to eat on the beach? Would he kiss her under Neptune's Arch until her knees buckled and she didn't even realise how itchy sand could be until the next day when her flesh ached for him?

No, he wouldn't. He wanted a bride he could keep at arm's length. She had got too close. Was that why he was running?

She folded her arms. 'Running never solves anything, Nico Del Castro.'

She'd run away once before and, if it hadn't been for Nico, she'd probably still be sitting in Villa Rosa staring out to sea and mourning her lost life. But Nico had made her see a world that existed outside class and discipline; he'd given her the new ingredients Bruno saw in her dancing. Life. Fire.

The truth was she'd been a coward. She saw that now. Too scared to confront her fears, her failure. If she'd just gone to Bruno in the first place maybe he'd have suggested a change of scenery anyway, helped her find a way to improve, and she could have spared herself all that heartache and uncertainty. But she'd been too lost, too heartbroken to risk opening up, to allow herself to be seen in all her vulnerability.

Not again.

No more regrets. She was going to tell Nico how she felt and if he didn't like it, didn't reciprocate, well, she'd lived through a broken heart before, she could do so again. But she wasn't going to just give up. Not this time. This time she was going to fight.

'You look ready for battle, Posy.'

Posy did her best to relax, unclenching her fists and remembering to smile, but she clearly wasn't fooling her family.

'I thought you were dancing Juliet, not Boudicca,' Immi teased.

'I'm just a little nervous.' She put on her most winning smile and beamed round at her family, who had been collected from Villa Rosa by palace drivers and were now gathered in one of the grand salons for an informal audience with Nico's family before the ball officially started. 'Don't you all scrub up nicely? Dad, you look so handsome in a tux.'

'I keep expecting someone to mistake me for a waiter,' her father confessed, pulling at his tie.

'If someone hands you a tray of canapés, then keep them,' Miranda told him. 'I'm starving. Will there be food later, Posy?'

'We already ate,' Immi reminded her twin, but Miranda just snorted.

'Hours ago so we could get ready for tonight and some of us are eating for two.'

'Don't worry, there are copious amounts of canapés and a whole room groaning with buffet food,' Posy assured her. 'The baby won't go hungry.'

She shifted, her nerves too tight to allow her to stay still. When could she get Nico alone? There were the family introductions to get through, after which they were heading straight to the September Ball, where Nico would be on the receiving line as a dutiful Crown Prince should, welcoming the island's great and good to the palace. Then, after the opening waltz they would announce her role as Patron of the Arts for the island and she would perform her solo, followed by Bruno's students. The chances of her speaking to Nico before midnight were slim but every second she didn't her fears and doubts grew. Was she just going to make a colossal fool of herself?

'It doesn't matter,' she reminded herself. 'It's time you learned to take a risk, remember?' But taking a risk was one thing, the slow build-up another, just like the agonising crawl up, up and up on a roller coaster, the eternal wait at the top of the loop with a sheer drop before you, knowing any moment now you were going to fall but with no idea when. Her stomach clenched with fear, her legs wobbled. She really needed to calm down somehow before she danced.

She wasn't sure how she made it through the next hour but despite her nerves it went surprisingly smoothly. Nico's mother had elected not to attend the ball so Posy was spared that particular introduction, and Javier's presence meant the usually haughty Queen was almost warm, unbending enough to make polite conversation with Posy's mother. The King, it turned out, had an interest in aviation and soon he and Posy's father were chatting away like old friends, joined by Cleve, Miranda and Imogen. The Dowager Queen had been frosty on introduction, obviously all too aware that these people knew and loved her greatest rival, but Portia used all her interviewing skills to break the ice and was soon entertaining the irascible old lady with outrageous titbits of Hollywood gossip.

Only Nico stood aloof, one hand on the ornate mantelpiece, looking more like a Regency hero than a real flesh and blood man, his features carved in stone, eyes set. Posy took a deep breath. They still had a job to do, people to fool, a relationship to fake. She walked over to him, smile steady and hands only a little shaky. 'I didn't imagine they would all get on so well.'

He didn't reply for a moment, the muscle in his cheek the only sign he was actually flesh and blood. 'Your family are lovely.'

'They have their moments,' she said thoughtlessly and winced. It was true they'd had their worries, her father's health this last year, Immi's troubles in her teen years, but they were still loving and supportive no matter what. Something Nico had never had. Something he was determined not to want, to need.

But no one could go through life alone.

Not even Nico.

You could say one thing about his timing: it totally sucked. Obviously he had had little choice. He needed Posy to accept the promotion as soon as possible, had to ensure his uncle didn't say anything about an engagement tonight, but playing the happy couple in such intimate surroundings, Posy's family clustered around them, was almost physically painful. The only thing he could do was turn off his feelings and detach himself from the whole situation.

Standing and watching the two families make their way through the stately dance of introductions, Nico felt more like an observer watching a play. Posy was coping better than he was—she was probably relieved the decision about her future had been made for her. She seemed a little nervy, her hands fluttering as she talked, her words a little fast, but that was to be expected. No doubt she was excited about her solo, about her future. Her freedom.

He'd have to keep an eye out, get tickets when she performed. Incognito, no royal box this time.

His uncle had frowned when Nico had informed him that they weren't planning to announce their engagement tonight and that Posy would be leaving L'Isola dei Fiori to take up her career once more, but had accepted the news with unexpected calm. 'I hope you haven't driven that girl away,' was all he'd said. 'She's far too good for you.'

'I know she is.' He'd left it at that. When his uncle found out the engagement was never going to happen he'd have the satisfaction of telling Nico that he'd told him so. Who was Nico to deprive him of that?

That detached feeling continued through the

early stages of the ball. He took his place in the line, grief stabbing him as he did so. This was Alessandro's place. As the spare, Nico had escaped the ordeal, using his time when he was younger to raid the buffet table, later on to chat up the prettier female guests. His parents, on the other hand, had always insisted on being included, needing that validation of their status. More fool them. An hour of shaking hands, remembering names and smiling at inanities left him with a headache and an urge for a strong drink. Instead he had to dance the first waltz. With Posy.

As she approached, shimmering in that dress, a goddess brought to earth, reality crashed back. His heart hammering, he took her hand, every nerve on fire where their flesh met. Her mouth was so soft, inviting, but not for him. Not any more.

But no one out there could suspect that they weren't in love, and so he made a sweeping bow, and allowed himself a teasing smile. 'My lady?'

Posy took his extended hand as she curtsied

with her usual grace. 'My Lord.' She paused. 'You can waltz, can't you? I don't want to dance Juliet with a bruised foot.'

'Waltz, foxtrot and tango,' he assured her. 'Part of the essential princely toolkit.'

His uncle and aunt had taken their place in the centre of the ballroom floor, his grandmother allowing a bristled field marshal to lead her out. Custom dictated that the first few turns would be made by the royal family alone, the rest of the guests joining in afterwards. The ballroom glittered, every chandelier lit, the sparkling lights reflecting off a thousand diamonds and other precious stones, myriad sequins and crystals on the gorgeous, jewel-like dresses of the assembled guests. Champagne was served in crystal flutes, the black dinner jackets of the men the only sombre note—although many were wearing waistcoats as gorgeous as any of the ladies' dresses. The September Ball was a time for colour, for celebration, and the island was known for its bright fabrics.

Posy's hand was cool in his as he put an arm

around her waist and drew her in close. He closed his eyes as he touched her supple curves, felt the heat of her through the thin fabric and inhaled her scent, a warm, spicy perfume. They had this one dance. He should make the most of it, a gift to himself, something to remember in the long years ahead.

'Are you having a nice time?' Oh, the inanity of that sentence. But what else could he say? I was wrong? Please don't go? Marry me, stay with me, love me. His jaw clenched.

'Not really.' Posy was still smiling, her voice low and intimate. For all the people watching them knew they were whispering love words to each other. They both knew how to play the game to perfection. At that moment the first chord swelled and the waltz began.

Neither spoke again. Nico knew he had been taught well and Posy was a dream to partner; she understood how to be led, how to respond, to follow his twists and turns with confidence and trust. The room fell away, the voices drowned out by the music until it was just the two of them in perfect time. Her hand in his, her breasts against his chest, hip to hip. It was all he could do not to pull her even closer, crush that soft mouth and claim her as his. Only his.

They should finish as they started. With a kiss. Only this time a goodbye kiss, a memory to keep him company through the years of duty and ritual that lay ahead.

Just one kiss…

The floor was filling up, laughing, smiling couples allowing themselves to be caught up in the romance of the moment. Nico navigated Posy around an elderly couple dancing in stately dignity and, without allowing himself to consider his actions, whisked her behind a curtain into a certain private alcove he had made good use of in years gone by, a low light and a small sofa making it the perfect secluded spot. They came to a stop, both breathing heavily, Posy's eyes glazed. 'What? Where? Why are we…?'

He didn't allow her to finish, couldn't allow her, pulling her closer as he had wanted to from the minute he'd seen her and kissing her with a force, a passion he hadn't allowed himself before. Not the teasing, gentle kisses or the carnal erotic embraces but pure want, pure need. A hard kiss, a punishing one, although who he wanted to punish he couldn't say. She froze for one moment and then her hands were around his neck, tangled in his hair, pulling him even closer.

'No...' She broke free, her hands pushing now so he staggered back, shocked.

What had he done?

'No,' Posy repeated. It couldn't be like this, not like this. Not anger and hurt and denial all mingling together. She had to tell him first, and then he could kiss her or walk away or take her right here against this wall; her knees buckled slightly and she put out a hand to steady herself.

His face whitened. 'I'm sorry. I shouldn't have. Forgive me.' He nodded, turned. And she knew if he went she would lose him for ever.

'No! Nico, don't go.' She grabbed his shoulder. 'Please. It wasn't that I didn't want you to kiss me. I did. I do. But there's something you need to know. I was going to say yes.'

He didn't move, his shoulders set, back rigid. 'I know. You have the chance to become a soloist. Congratulations, Posy, I know you'll be magnificent.'

'No,' she said again, feeling a little like a foolish parrot. 'I mean, yes, Bruno has asked me to return and offered me the opportunity to dance solo roles but I haven't answered him yet. I was going to say yes to you. To staying. To marrying you.'

He quivered then, a movement so slight that if she weren't so finely attuned to him she might have missed it. Slowly, slowly he turned back to face her. The alcove was small, almost oppressive, the thick velvet curtain shielding them from the ballroom. They were in a world of their own.

'Why? Bruno offered you everything you want. Everything you've worked for. Why throw that away?'

It was time. Posy took a deep breath, hands

clenched, her nails biting into her palms. 'Not quite everything. He didn't offer me you.'

The silence stretched around them. Nico's gaze was intent on hers, his eyes darker than the sea at midnight. 'Me?'

'Three months ago all I wanted was a solo. I didn't want anyone or anything else. But then I met you.'

He didn't respond. She took a small step closer.

'I've never done anything like that before. That first night on the beach. I told myself it was be-cause I was lonely—and I was—and lost. I was that too but that's not why. I did it because you were the most beautiful man I'd ever seen and I was so tired of being afraid, of not reaching out, of not living. And so I did, and the consequences were catastrophic. I embarrassed my family, your family, turned your life upside down. But you never blamed me. Didn't leave me to deal with the consequences I brought on myself. You were honourable and kind and protected me. Just like you protect the island and everyone on it. Put-ting yourself last.'

Another step. They were almost back in waltz position, barely a millimetre between them. 'I knew what you were offering, Nico, and it seemed fair. I didn't expect to fall in love with you. I've never been in love before, you see. But I did. I am. And that's why I was going to say yes and stay. I don't expect you to love me back. I know that's not the deal. But I needed you to know that. Before I leave. You're a good man, Nico. My heart is safe with you.'

His expression was shuttered. 'I'm not good or honourable. I let Alessandro down. I let you down. I should have swum away that night, not dragged you into this life.'

'No, no you didn't let me down and you certainly didn't let Alessandro down. Your cousin never expected you to give up your life and dreams for him. Talk to Guido—listen to him. Alessandro would never have abdicated even if you had offered to take over. He was always ready to do his duty no matter what the cost. As for me. You didn't let me down, you saved me.'

She scanned his face. Had she got through?

Was he going to walk away, horrified by the emotion? She could barely breathe as he just looked at her.

And then he touched her. One fleeting caress, a hand on her cheek, his finger brushing her mouth. Her skin sizzled where he touched. 'That night I was facing up to the reality of my life here. I'd managed to bury it, the last two years, pouring everything into my MBA, not grieving Alessandro, not allowing myself to think about what being Crown Prince really entailed. And then I found myself back here with a diary full of engagements, an earful of admonishments from my uncle, a realisation that all control over my life had gone. I gave myself one last evening, away from my bodyguards, away from the palace. It was a farewell to my life. And then I saw you... I thought I had conjured you up, a naiad from beneath the waves.'

Posy smiled then, knowing her heart was in her eyes. 'I'm all too real.'

'Yes,' he said hoarsely. 'You are. And you're too good for me. I can't allow you to give up your dreams for me, Posy.'

'Nico, do you love me?'

She couldn't breathe while she waited for him to answer. And then he bowed his head so their foreheads touched, his hands light on her shoulders. 'Yes. I really do. Madly. So much I tried to let you go.'

Tears ran down Posy's cheeks; she hadn't even noticed her eyes filling, the lump in her throat. 'For an intelligent man, Nico Del Castro, you can be very stupid.'

'You're sure, Posy? It's a lot, this life of mine. As Crown Princess, as Queen, you'll always have to put L'Isola dei Fiori first, never have a life that's truly your own. Can you cope with that?'

'If you're with me, then yes. I can cope with anything.'

He smiled then, suddenly younger, carefree, once more the dangerously sexy man on the beach. 'In that case, Posy Marlowe...' he reached into his pocket and brought out a small, dark blue leather box '...would you do me the very great honour of being my Princess, my future Queen, but, most importantly, my wife?'

EPILOGUE

Ten months later

'READY, POSY? HER father fiddled nervously with his collar. King Vincenzo had invested him with an honorary military title and he was uncomfortably wearing the uniform to match. Her parents had also been granted titles and were now the Conte and Contessa of Baia de Rose, to their slight embarrassment.

'Ready,' she confirmed, looking at herself in the mirror. This was the last time she would be simply Posy Marlowe. In an hour's time she would be Rosalind Del Castro, Crown Princess of L'Isola dei Fiori. She would be a wife. 'I don't think I can add anything else, do you?'

Her dress was probably a little more ornate than she would have personally chosen. She'd been aware that she needed to stand out in the old medieval cathedral, that her wedding wasn't a personal ceremony but a way of putting L'Isola dei Fiori on the map. Posy had decided on a sweetheart neckline, the skirt swelling out just a little, enough to give her some presence, the whole dress covered with delicate pearls. A lacy overdress covered her shoulders for the ceremony and then cascaded down her back and into a train long enough for her six bridesmaids to carry—and crucially she could remove it during the reception so she would be able to dance unencumbered. The Del Castro diamonds adorned her neck, earlobes and wrists and a magnificent tiara held her long veil in place.

'You look so beautiful,' her father told her. 'Even more beautiful than you looked in Giselle.'

Posy squeezed his hand. Nico had insisted that she went back to London for one last year to seize her opportunity to dance some solos and featured roles. A steady winter dancing bit parts had led to the opportunity to dance bigger roles over the spring and early summer, culminating in several matinee performances as the coveted lead including Giselle. She was leaving the stage behind with no regrets, no dreams left unfulfilled.

Ahead of her lay the excitement of introducing dance and drama to the island, into the schools and the newly restored theatre. Their engagement and wedding had pulled tourists to the island in their thousands and she knew she and Nico had an important role in ensuring that they returned and brought their friends and families with them. From next week the first few lucky guests would be staying at the luxuriously renovated Villa Rosa—but for the next few days the cliff-top house would be home to her and Nico alone. Their very own idyll. After all, it was thanks to her godmother's legacy that they had met on that moonlit night nearly one year ago...

'Okay then, let's do this.'

She turned and smiled at her sisters and mother. They were all in blue, the colour of the sea that had brought her Nico, her mother smart in a dress and matching jacket, a huge hat balanced on her head, her sisters in long straight gowns. Her other bridesmaids, including Daria, were already in the first of the three horse-drawn carriages that would convey her and her entourage to the cathedral.

Immi held a beautiful bouquet, but Miranda and Portia were holding bundles far more precious: Miranda's eight-month-old daughter, Daisy, in a gorgeous blue and white dress, ballet slippers on her chubby feet, while Portia cradled her tiny little girl. Just a few weeks old, Isabelle was maybe a little young to be a bridesmaid but there was no way Posy was leaving her newest niece out of the wedding party. Her father looked at his family, his heart in his eyes. For all he joked about being horribly outnumbered by the womenfolk, Posy knew he wouldn't have it any other way. Besides, as Immi pointed out, he wasn't alone any more with three—soon to be four—sons-in-law.

Immi was smiling softly at the babies. She and Matt had decided that they would give IVF a chance and she would be starting treatment soon. Posy hoped it would be successful, but she knew their relationship was strong enough to weather any storm and disappointment.

'We'd better get going,' Portia said a little gruffly, wiping away a tear. 'A bride doesn't get to be fashionably late when there's TV cameras involved.'

'Okay.' Posy embraced her mother and sisters one more time and then she allowed her father to hand her up into the open carriage. The journey passed like a dream, the waving and cheering crowds lining the streets a mirage, and soon she was standing at the back of the long cathedral aisle, her skirt shaken out and adjusted, her train in one perfect line, her father solemn as they began their procession to the altar—and to Nico.

Her heart turned as she saw him, grave and handsome in his own military uniform, the medals glittering on his chest. They were both so dressed up, more like characters in a film than real people. But as he caught her eye, as his own eyes widened in appreciation and a smile spread over his face, he winked. Just a small wink, a reminder that, at the end of the day, they were just two people who loved each other. And as Posy began to recite the vows that would make her his wife she knew that that was all that mattered.

* * * * *

If you loved this book,
make sure you catch the rest
of the SUMMER AT VILLA ROSA *quartet!*

HER PREGNANCY BOMBSHELL
by Liz Fielding
THE MYSTERIOUS ITALIAN HOUSEGUEST
by Scarlet Wilson
THE RUNAWAY BRIDE AND THE
BILLIONAIRE
by Kate Hardy

Available now!